Jack Boys vs Dope Boys 3

Romell Tukes

Lock Down Publications and Ca$h
Presents
JACK BOYS VS. DOPE BOYS 3
A Novel by *Romell Tukes*

Romell Tukes

Lock Down Publications
P.O. Box 944
Stockbridge, Ga 30281
www.lockdownpublications.com

Copyright 2022 by Romell Tukes
Jack Boys Vs. Dope Boys 3

This is a work of fiction. Names, characters, places, and incidents either are products of the author's imagination or are used fictitiously. Any similarity to actual events or locales or persons, living or dead, is entirely coincidental.

Lock Down Publications
Like our page on Facebook: Lock Down Publications @
www.facebook.com/lockdownpublications.ldp

Book interior design by: **Shawn Walker**
Edited by: **Jill Alicea**

Stay Connected with Us!

Text **LOCKDOWN** to 22828 to stay up-to-date with new releases, sneak peaks, contests and more…

Thank you!

Submission Guideline.

Submit the first three chapters of your completed manuscript to ldpsubmissions@gmail.com, subject line: Your book's title. The manuscript must be in a .doc file and sent as an attachment. Document should be in Times New Roman, double spaced and in size 12 font. Also, provide your synopsis and full contact information. If sending multiple submissions, they must each be in a separate email.

Have a story but no way to send it electronically? You can still submit to LDP/Ca$h Presents. Send in the first three chapters, written or typed, of your completed manuscript to:

LDP: Submissions Dept
P.O. Box 944
Stockbridge, Ga 30281

DO NOT send original manuscript. Must be a duplicate.

Provide your synopsis and a cover letter containing your full contact information.

Thanks for considering LDP and Ca$h Presents.

Acknowledgements

First and foremost, I would like to always give praise to Allah. Thanks to my real family and friends. Big thank you to all the readers with the positive feedback and good vibes, thanks for the support and push. Shout out to my city 914 area, Yonkers, Peck, MV, you know the vibes. Shout to CB, Frazier, Lingo, YB, Moreno, Baby James and DT from Yonkers. Shout to my Brooklyn people, OG Chuck, Gunny, Tails, Lil YB from Brownsville, Tim Dog from Bed-Stuy and Black Knowledge. Shout to Dax from S.I. Shout Spice and Double O from Newburg, NY Shout to my N.C. and Atlanta niggas. Texas, Miami and the West Coast, you know the vibes. I am the Hov of the pen game, #Big Facts, hate it or love it. Free da real and shoot for the stars and don't let your dreams face away. Don't let a hater choke your vision. Good energy and good vibes. Reach out to me on my Facebook page, Bama Author from New York City, NY and on my IG @RomellTheAuthor. Thank you and enjoy.

Romell Tukes

Jack Boys vs Dope Boys

Prologue

After a long few months of dealing with all the drama in the Bronx, Knight was finally able to look back on things and think clearly. Beefing with Khalid was an uphill task people were trying to get at him daily. Luckily, Khalid's most dangerous daughter, Behadi, crossed sides because she fell in love with Lil K. Having Behadi's help was like a miracle in so many ways. Killing Khalid eventually was a big weight off all of their shoulders at the end.

Uncle P, Gotti, and Khalid being all brothers was the biggest shock to everybody. Uncle P was sending his best trained whores at Knight and his crew, but they didn't stand a chance against Knight's crew. When Uncle P had Red kidnapped, he turned her into his personal sex slave and killer by brainwashing her and putting a spell on her. Every time Red used to see Lil K, old feelings used to come back. Even though she lost most of her memory, she could never forget about the only man she loved. When Red killed Uncle P, it ended their beef. She found Lil K and he witnessed her kill herself. Seeing her kill herself crushed him and he had to live with the hurt even though he had moved on with Behadi.

Lil K's new recruit, Balla, was taking his old worker's position in the crew because J. Balla had a name in the Bronx like his brother M. Balla. M Balla had Castle Hill and Sandview under his wing and basically most of the South Bronx.

Since Knight met the Costa Rican sisters, he'd been focused on bigger and better things. Finding out who Gotti's wife was, Knight couldn't believe it. The day he killed Gotti, his life changed for good.

Bree was becoming a big problem, snaking everybody she got close to - even Knight.

Smoke pretended to be Knight's and Lil K's father until his cover was blown, but before he got killed, he let out a big secret. Smoke let Knight know that Jose Martinez killed his father years ago when he was a kid.

Now that Knight and his Bronx crew were down with Rachela, they had big plans to get to a bigger bag. When Rachela kidnapped his daughter and baby mother, he had no choice but to agree with her madness and let her supply him with drugs. After she let his family go, he moved them to Texas and crossed over at the right time.

With D Fatal Brim home in L.A., Knight thought his boy would reach out to him and keep in touch, but he did the opposite.

Rachela and Aliza, both Jose Martinez's daughters, were on a mission to please their father, but things didn't go as planned.

With so many enemies at the time, Knight ain't know what angle to come at his opps at until he met MeMe, a woman he had no clue was a Queenpin until she killed Bree and her seed. Joining MeMe was the best thing he knew he could have done because he trusted her energy. MeMe's sister Keiline had a baby with Wolf, but MeMe was strictly on her business and she didn't play any games.

Going through so much drama and losing so many good men, Knight hoped this would be a new start, even though the Cubans were still heavy on his mind.

Jack Boys vs Dope Boys

Chapter 1
Bronx, NY

Knight was standing in the meat factory in Hunts Point he had just opened with Lil K months ago. The factory packaged, shipped, and delivered meat all around the world. Most would think this was a legit business like the clubs Knight had opened, but that wasn't this establishment. Knight was getting kilos packed into tons of meat from pigs, cows, chicken, shark meat, and any type of meat you can think of.

MeMe kept her word and was sending Knight the most work he ever got in his life, and the product was locking down the whole city. Teaming up with the Costa Rican woman was the best thing that ever happened to him. They had a strictly business relationship with each other and it was like the sexual vibe they once shared never happened. Knight preferred business rather than sex with any woman because pussy comes once a nigga gets the bag. He learned that early in the game.

Trucks backed into the warehouse, which was freezing cold as workers unloaded trucks, having no clue they were moving pounds of coke from 18 wheeler to 18 wheeler.

Meeting the kid Wolf was cool. He liked his style and he saw how he was really business-minded. He had to give it to Wolf for bagging a bad bitch like Keiline. She was a dime model type, just like MeMe. To see two bad bitches run their own empire, he respected it, and they were about their business.

Last year was stressful for Knight. He saw his hard work slipping out of his hands. Going against Khalid, an African drug lord, Gotti, a kingpin from VA, and Uncle Pimp and his whores, was tearing him down. Luckily he had a man who claimed to be his father step in the picture and try to supply him with drugs.

The man who played his dad was Smoke, but that didn't last for long. Smoke's own wife Rachela tried to backdoor Smoke and blackmail Knight by kidnapping his baby mother and daughter. Knight fell for her trick, but when Smoke died, he told Knight he wasn't his real dad. He told Knight his father was killed by Rachela's father, a Cuban boss named Jose Martinez.

Once Knight got all the information he needed, he cut Rachela off and killed his enemy with the help of his crew. Things were a little different now because the only enemy he knew of was the Cubans.

Knight left Hunts Point, on his way to the gym. It was summertime in a few weeks so he wanted to get back in shape. Last month he bought a new mansion in Fishkill, NY but he also had another house in Long Island and two condos in the city.

Finding out his late brother Kazzy had a son with Julie was still surprising to him. Knight had not heard from Julie since he left her home after trying to ask her for help with the Cubans. He tried to call the jail D Fatal Brim was at to pay him a visit, but he wasn't there. Knight tried to look him up, but he wasn't in the system, which didn't make sense. Knight knew if D Fatal Brim would have won his appeal and got released he would have reached out to him. He only hoped his boy was okay and safe.

Next week Lil K was getting married in Puerto Rico to Behadi and he was happy for his little brother. Lil K had been through a tough road so Knight knew he deserved happiness. Behadi was the most official chick he ever met so he knew she would be the one for him. Knight couldn't be happier for Lil K. He planned to show up single because he had no woman at the time. He was too busy to entertain a relationship.

Chapter 2
Coamo, Puerto Rico

Lil K had rented a big house on a beach for the small wedding he was having today. He only invited Knight, J Balla, and a few childhood friends from the Bronx. Behadi had one of her friends as a bridesmaid and that was all because he was her only family now. She had killed her own family to save him.

Knight was watching his little brother get ready, thinking how he grew up so fast.

"You look nervous," Knight said as Lil K turned to look at him.

"Who?"

"You too fucking big to be an owl," Knight joked.

"Hell yeah, I'm nervous. Nigga, I'm 'bout to marry a trained killer, bro. What if she catch me cheating?"

"She gonna shoot your dick off, nigga," Knight joked.

"Nigga, I'm serious," Lil K said, putting on the Richard Muller watch he'd only worn twice.

"Bro, when you get married, you take an oath to give her your all and give up your desires," Knight said, standing up.

"I love her. I just don't want to hurt her."

"So, you're not ready?"

"I am. I just want to make sure I hold my oath to her bro because I know she deserves it, son," Lil K stated, putting out his prayer rug.

"Facts. I'm proud of you."

"Thanks."

"Don't thank me. Thank Allah. I'm going to let you make your salat," Knight said, leaving the room to go check on Behadi, who he had a closer relationship with.

Lil K was having a Muslim wedding since he and Behadi were both Muslims. He knew Behadi was the right one for him since he first laid eyes on her in Africa The only problem then was that he was with Red, who had been the love of his life for years. Once Red got kidnapped by Uncle Pimp, his life changed. When Uncle Pimp brainwashed Red and gave her HIV, the game plan changed. The night Red killed Uncle Pimp, she realized her life was now over, but she went to hunt down Lil K and found him eventually. Lil K's newborn with Behadi was killed by Money, who popped up and disappeared as fast as he came back. The death of his child hurt him so when he ran into Red in the back of his projects, Millbrook in the Bronx, he was numb to any feelings. After talking to her for a brief second, he walked off to hear a gunshot. He turned around to see that Red had killed herself.

When he got done praying, he took a shot of Dom. P and thought about how crazy his life had been since his mom got killed. With forty minutes left before the wedding began, he closed his eyes and took a deep breath.

***

Behadi was applying a little makeup, but not too much because she didn't want to overdo it. She looked beautiful today in her $850,000 dress and $2.7 million worth of diamonds on her body. The thought of getting married today hadn't hit her yet. Lil K made her so happy he treated her like the African queen she was, and she loved him for it.

Losing her child at the hands of Money took a lot out of her. Even though she killed Bree, who was Money's baby mother, and their child, she still felt empty. It's hard for any woman to lose a child she carried in her womb for nine months.

"Behadi," a voice outside the door stated, and she knew it was Knight.

"Come in, Knight."

"Damn, sister-in-law, you looking like a snack. Lil K better watch out," he joked, sitting down.

"Boy, you so stupid." She laughed hard.

"You ready?"

"As I can be," she replied.

"Okay."

"You think he ready for this, Knight?"

"Yeah. If he wasn't, he wouldn't have dragged you out here. You know my brother," Knight said as she nodded her head.

"True."

"It's almost time. I'll meet you outside, big head. Hurry up, and don't be up in here crying and shit," Knight said, laughing.

"Boy, shut up."

Behadi continued to get ready for her big day. She couldn't stop thinking about the night Lil K proposed to her in Manhattan. She was always scared of heights, so when he proposed to her on one of the highest sky rises in Manhattan, she almost passed out on him, especially after seeing the diamond ring.

Romell Tukes

Jack Boys vs Dope Boys

Chapter 3
Coamo, Puerto Rico

Behadi walked down the white sand beach with Knight on her arm as he was her maid of honor. Lil K waited for her next to his boy M Balla's brother J Balla, who took over M Balla's position. There was an older Muslim man standing in front of them with a noble Qu'ran in his right hand. Behadi couldn't stop smiling as she was face to face with her lover.

The Imam (Muslim leader) opened the Qu'ran and started reading them their vows. Lil K saw Behadi cry and his eyes got glossy. It only took five minutes for the Imam to give his ceremony before Lil K placed the big diamond ring on her finger. When they kissed and the loud music played, they were now finally married. Behadi turned around to say something to her friend when she caught movement in the house. Everybody was outside and nobody was inside, so she knew something was very wrong.

"It's a hit!" Behadi yelled seeing over forty shooters flood the area.

Tat! Tat! Tat! Tat! Tat! Tat! Tat! Tat!

Behadi's friend and the Muslim Imam got hit up because they moved too slowly to take cover. Lil K, Knight, and J Balla pulled out their guns, firing at the large group of Cuban men with Cuban flags on their heads and faces.

"Take Behadi to the boat!" Knight yelled to Lil K as Knight and J Balla tried to take out as many gunmen as possible.

Bloc! Bloc! Bloc! Bloc! Bloc! Bloc!

The boat was there for Lil K and Behadi's honeymoon, but now it was the getaway.

"It's too many of them, son," J Balla yelled, hitting two of the shooters.

Bloc! Bloc! Bloc!

Tat! Tat! Tat! Tat! Tat!

Knight saw Rachela standing on the balcony of the mansion in a sexy wedding dress watching the whole scene.

Bloc! Bloc! Bloc!

Knight fired three shots at her, then he and J Balla got on the boat before more and more Cubans arrived to kill them.

"Yo, what the fuck!" J Balla had never seen anything like that in the Bronx.

"Who was that?" Lil K asked, driving the boat.

"The Cubans," Knight said, watching the mansion from a distance.

"They tried to ruin my big day," Behadi said, upset that she almost got hit and that she left her gun upstairs.

"That was Rachela. I haven't seen her since I cut her off to deal with MeMe," Knight stated.

"So she back for blood, huh?" J Balla asked.

"Yeah." Knight wished he would have killed her before because he had a feeling she was coming back hard.

"How did she know we were here?" Lil K asked out loud but not talking to anybody.

"She smart, bro, but don't worry. We gonna get them," Knight stated, meaning every word.

Chapter 4
Compton, Los Angeles

D Fatal Brim posted on a dangerous block most called 400 block. The block was full of Piru blood gangbangers. D Fatal Brim was treated like royalty even though he repped a different set Brim gang.

Big Bo ran 400 block and he had been close friends with D Fatal Brim for years. The two met in the federal prison and got close. Big Bo had the west coast Bloods and D Fatal Brim controlled the East coast Bloods. Big Bo went home and kept in touch with D Fatal Brim, so it was only right for him to get up with Big Bo when he moved to Los Angeles. When D Fatal Brim told Big who his wife was, he had no clue he was connected to the Cherry Valley Cartel run by Marie. D Fatal Brim supplied Big Bo and his Piru gang with keys and they showed him love. Marie already had gangs of Mexicans all across the city under her control, but no black gangs like the Crips and Bloods until now.

Since coming home, life had been different for him. Marie introduced him to this new life of riches and he fell in love with it. He had no clue Marie was living so good while he was locked away. Til this day, he counted his blessings meeting her on a dating site. Marrying her was the best thing that ever happened to him in his life. The only downfall was he had to pick a side when he came home from prison after giving his life sentence back. Marie made him pick hers or Knight's crew because there was a war going on and Marie needed to know whose side her husband was going to be on. Luckily, he chose her side, but Knight never betrayed him; only treated him with love. If it wasn't for Knight getting Mita, the head District Attorney at the time, to file a motion to dismiss his case, he would never be here. The betrayal ate him every day, but he couldn't turn on Marie. He missed New York, but Los Angeles was just as much fun, if not more. The only issue was his east coast set, but Big Bo had a lot of respect in the hoods from L.B.C. to Crenshaw.

"Whoop." Big Bo came out from the back of the house in a tank top, jeans, and red Chuck Taylor with red laces. Big Bo was a big baldheaded man with big muscles and jailhouse tattoos.

"What's poppin?"

"My bad it took so long. I was lifting weights with the little homies back there," Big Bo said, making his chest jump.

"I see, Blood." D Fatal Brim laughed at his homie.

"I got da paper for you too."

Big Bo looked at a cute, light-skinned woman sitting on the porch. The woman saw the look and went into the house.

"A'ight, but how's business?"

"Shit good, Blood. I got some shit going on with the Rolling 60's Crips. They buying from me now," Big Bo stated.

"Okay, that's what's up, son. But what's up with the east coast Crips? I thought you said they wanted to get down?" D Fatal Brim remembered Big Bo talking about them a few days ago when he came out here.

"Them fools heard I was doing business with the 60's and said they good," Big Bo told him as the woman came out with a big duffle bag.

"Damn, why?"

"Them niggas hate the 60's, Bloods. You ain't know?"

"Nah."

"They rivals, bro," Big Bo said as he saw the light-skinned chick place the money in D Fatal Brim's Bentley coupe.

"Fuck it."

"I'm going to get up with the Stones later to see if them niggas ready to end this beef and get money," Big Bo said, smoking a blunt of weed as the police rode by them.

"Y'all got beef?"

"Hell yeah."

"When that shit start?" D Fatal Brim asked, not knowing Big Bo had beef with the P. Stones.

"Them niggas killed the little homie two years ago and shit been litty ever since," Big Bo said.

"They in the jungle?"

"Yeah. Them niggas got that shit trapped off. Blood."

"They get money?" D Fatal Brim wanted to know.

"Big money, Blood."

"Well, make that move, son. We trying to lock shit down."

"I'm with you," Big Bo said.

"A'ight, I'm going to have my people call you when they ready to drop off," D Fatal Brim said.

"Don't send them crazy-ass Avenue niggas again," Big Bo said.

"A'ight." D Fatal Brim laughed because last shipment, the Avenue boys hit two of Big Bo's homies with their car, killing them by mistake because they were drunk driving.

Romell Tukes

Chapter 5
Harlem, NY

Spanish Harlem to Harlem was run by a man they called OG, a black and Cuban man who was so low key only one of his workers saw him. OG escaped from a New York State prison years ago with the help of his girlfriend, Maryanna, a sexy Dominican woman.

While in prison he was with son CB, who was Wolf's brother, but OG never told CB he was his dad until later on. Wolf's mom Rita and OG used to be lovers until she snitched on OG and got him life in prison.

Wolf's aunt had a low key relationship with OG for years. He had her kill his lawyer, judge, and any serious threats. He had been planning his escape since his first day in prison. Now he was a free man and he had to enjoy life, but he still had to hustle.

OG's capo was Rocky. He was the one moving his weight all through Harlem and Spanish Harlem. Maryanna got him a new Social Security number, name, birthdate, and all. If she could buy him new DNA she would. When Maryanna wasn't in Harlem with him, she was in the Dominican Republic doing her own thing.

OG had a nice apartment uptown, but this was one of many he had in the city. He sat in his living room smoking a cigar, thinking about the man who murdered his son. Wolf murdered his son, which was Wolf's blood brother, in a war, and OG wanted revenge. Word was Wolf had Yonkers in a chokehold and there was a lot of money going through that small town. OG also heard Wolf had from Yonkers all the way up to Buffalo on lock and he wanted in. He had Rocky on it trying to figure out Wolf's operations, but Rocky said he needed more time because Wolf was smart.

***

South Bronx, NY

J Balla drove through his city with his top down on his BMW coupe, listening to a Brooklyn rapper named 22gz. Since coming back from Puerto Rico, he'd been on his money pickups. He had workers all over the Bronx from Uptown, west side, and the south Bronx. When it came to picking up his money, he did that himself.

J Balla couldn't shake the thought out of his head about what took place at Lil K's wedding a few days ago. He had never been ambushed like that and to have a shootout at Lil K's wedding was some real disrespectful shit. The crazy shit was when he saw a bad Spanish bitch in a wedding dress watching the scene from the balcony like she was the female *Scarface*.

Lil K was overseas so he knew calling him today wasn't going to happen but J Balla needed to re-up. J Balla had a little over eighty keys left and he knew that would only last two days or less. Stopping at a red light on his way to Highbridge he looked at the tattoo of his brother on his arm.

M Balla was his blood brother, so when he got killed, J Balla was on Rikers Island jail hurting. The brothers grew up in the Castle Hill section they had on lock for years. J Balla was a Blood, so his crew was making big noise in the Bronx. The city made Knight at least a million dollars every other week.

When he got to Highbridge projects, he saw a few goons on the block. Everybody in Highbridge worked for an older nigga named Science, who worked for J Balla.

"Yo, call Science for me, son," J Balla said, getting out of his car with his weapon tucked.

"A'ight," one of the young men said, running into the building.

Minutes later a big, cocky, dark-skinned nigga came out with a scar across his face and a bald head. "Peace," Science said, approaching J Balla.

Science was God body. He thought he was God, and he would always talk science to niggas in the hood, but nobody wanted to hear that shit. J Balla did a bid with Science and he came home and ran into Science who was down bad. Seeing how broke and fucked up he was he gave him a chance to get some real money. Now Science pushed a G-Wagon Benz SUV.

"What's up?"

"You back. How was your trip, god?" Science asked, sniffing.

"It was cool, but some brazy shit went down bro," J Balla said.

"That's crazy."

"Yeah, but it is what it is, bro," J Balla said.

"Facts."

"What's up with that loot?" J Balla rubbed his hands together, wondering why Science ain't come out with no bag.

"Something happened," Science stated sadly.

"I'm not understanding." J Balla's look was confused.

"I got robbed a few days ago. Some Mexicans - I mean Jamaicans - took everything," Science said, nervously shaking.

J Balla paused, wondering how a nigga got Mexicans and Jamaicans confused. None of the shit was making sense to him. "How come you ain't call me?" J Balla asked.

"They took my phone," Science said, forgetting he had his iPhone on his hip.

J Balla laughed and pulled out his phone to make a call. Months ago he heard that Science had a drug problem but he didn't care as long as Science had his money every trip. Science heard his phone ring and picked it up.

"Hold on, J Balla," Science said, turning around to talk to whoever was calling.

"It's me, dumbass," J Balla said, on the phone as niggas were watching the scene, shaking their heads being nose.

Science knew he fucked up when J Balla pulled his gun out and aimed it to his face.

"Where's my money?" J Balla's face tightened.

"I'll get it."

"Where is it?"

"I fucked up," Science said in tears.

"You smoked it?"

"I sniffed some – well, most of it. I'm sorry, son, I'll make it right. I'll——"

Bloc! Bloc! Bloc! Bloc! Bloc! Bloc!

J Balla shot him six times in the face, killing him.

"I'll be back in a few days. I want one of you young niggas to take over for this fiend-ass nigga," J Balla said, pulling off.

Romell Tukes

Chapter 6
Hollywood, CA

Marie loved the view of her crib. It was a beautiful sight of the Hollywood sign in the mountains of the city. This was the city she loved so much and couldn't get enough of, but now she had the gang of L.A. on her side. D Fatal Brim was making power moves in L.A. with the Crips and the Bloods. She had no clue her husband knew so many people. He was connected to the streets and she was connected to the cartels. Having her husband home meant so much to her because he was that piece she was missing in life.

Marie had a bigger problem than L.A. right now. The Costa Rican sisters recently killed one of her main clients from another cartel family in Mexico. Marie wanted to network into Vegas, Texas, and Arizona because she already had people in almost every other state on the west coast. D Fatal Brim was out in the streets setting up a truce with the Rolling 60's Crips and the east coast Crips so they could get money. Marie hadn't yet told her husband about the war that was soon to go up in flames.

***

South Miami, FL

Dussa was the new face to certain hoods in South Miami like Liberty City, Carol City, and the South Beach area. Dussa worked for the biggest queenpin in the state of Florida or maybe the whole south, a woman named Julie. Dussa had been in the game for ten years now and he rose in the ranks from the bottom to the top. Working for a person like Julie was very dangerous if one would ever cross her.

Dussa was a handsome Puerto Rican. He found Julie very, very attractive but with her, it was all business or nothing. He moved bricks all through Miami with his crew. Dussa dealt with the low class Cubans, Haitians, and the blacks. Today he met a new client named Tito. He was a Cuban man from Lil Havana known for its high population of Cubans. Dussa knew Julie hated dealing with

Cubans, but he had a drop off for 250 keys and he wasn't going to miss that.

***

Lil Havana, Miami

Today was blazing hot outside but it was normal to every Miami resident. Dussa came alone. He pulled up to a small house that had two big Spanish men on the porch as watchguards. This was Dussa's first time doing business in this area because it didn't belong to him or Julie, so he stayed away. Julie wasn't the only big-time plug Miami. There were a few big other names in the 305.

Getting out of his car, he walked up to the porch.

"Tito?" Dussa asked.

"Backyard, my friend," one of the men replied.

"Okay."

Walking through the house, he saw women and men cooking and bagging up drugs. Once in the backyard, he saw Tito in a nice Versace button-up, wearing shades and smiling.

"Dussa, good to see you." Tito smiled, getting up to shake the man's hand.

"Same to you. This is a nice little set up back here," Dussa said, looking around at the outdoor bar and small pool area.

"I like to have a little fun even while on business. Thanks for coming out," Tito said, taking off his shades.

"Sure, I'm always down to do good business," Dussa said.

"Okay, so let's talk. I need 250 keys."

"That's not an issue. I have it ready as we speak." Dussa smiled, knowing this deal would be easy.

"Good, but first, I must tell you there is something I have to tell you." Tito's smile vanished.

"What's that?" Dussa felt a weird vibe.

Tito whistled and eight of his workers rushed out with all types of assault rifles. Dussa had got set up and he felt dumb for slipping, all because of greed.

"You set me up."

"Not really. It wasn't me. It was her," Tito said, seeing a beautiful woman come out the back door carrying a Draco.

"Who the fuck is she?" Dussa wanted to know, seeing a bad bitch in a dress.

"I'll answer that, papi. I'm Aliza. I'm with the Martinez Cartel from Cuba," Aliza said, sitting down, staring at Dussa.

"What is this about?" Dussa asked.

"Not you, papi. Don't overwhelm yourself. But you work for Julie and let's just say you got caught in the crossfire," Aliza told him honestly.

"I see. So you think I'm gonna give up Julie?"

"No, you're too loyal, so I'm just going to kill you and send her your body." Aliza was nonchalant about the whole thing.

"What's the hold up?" Dussa said.

"I like you. I wish you could have been on my side," Aliza stated, looking at Tito then Dussa.

"Too bad, huh," Tito said.

"Did I ask you to speak?" Aliza asked Tito, her worker.

"Sorry," Tito replied before Aliza turned her weapon on Dussa.

Tat! Tat! Tat! Tat! Tat! Tat! Tat! Tat!

Dussa's body flipped out of the chair.

***

Dade County, FL

Julie got a call from her guards at the gate asking her to come to the front gate for a second. She hated getting up early in the morning. She would normally get up around 11 a.m.

Miami was hers. She'd been making power moves and networking all throughout the south in Alabama, Atlanta, Kentucky, Little Rock, New Orleans, and Nashville, TN. She was very busy nowadays and since losing her son she hadn't been able to snap back to her old self.

Being a mother used to be amazing to her. She was overprotective and didn't play with her baby, so losing him took a toll on her. Every time she would look at her son she saw Kazzy,

29

the child's father, who was Knight's late brother. She hadn't seen Knight since he came to Miami to ask her about the Cubans, whom she has been at war with for some time now.

Walking outside, she saw a lot of commotion and as she got closer to the gate she saw why everybody was going crazy. Dussa's lifeless body was hanging from her gate with a Cuban flag tied to his head. Julie knew it was the Martinez Cartel, mainly Rachela or Aliza, one of the sisters who had been trying to take over Miami for years. Dussa was a good and loyal worker. She felt upset for his death. She knew death was a part of the game but she hated to lose good men on her watch.

"Take him down," Julie told the guards surrounding the dead body watching.

She walked inside, thinking it was war time because she wasn't going to let that slide. Julie decided right then she would call Knight and give him a helping hand. She knew Knight like the back of her hand and when he had an enemy, he wouldn't stop until they were dead. Julie also knew he would need as much help as possible with the Cubans.

First she had to move, because they knew where she lived. Since MeMe informed her that Rachela killed her son, she'd been trying to come up with a plan to get back, but she was still dwelling on the loss of her only child.

Chapter 7
Alajoda, Costa Rica

Knight walked into the beautiful home that belonged to MeMe. Four large men led him into the mansion to a nice and large living room area with expensive artwork on the walls. MeMe had asked him to come out for the weekend, so he took the first flight to Costa Rica.

"Knight, how are you doing?" MeMe said, coming from down the wrap stairs.

"What's up, MeMe?" Knight saw how beautiful she looked in all white.

"I got the chefs cooking up some soul food for you. Would you like anything else?" she asked.

"Nah, that's more than enough," he told her.

"Are you sure? I can have him put some more food on," she said before sitting down.

"Thank you, but I'm okay. How many houses you got out here?" he asked, because he came to a new one every time he would come to visit her.

"Three out here and two in the States."

"Oh, that's cool. But why you need to see me?" he asked.

"I ain't need to see you. I wanted to see you." Her tone of voice had Knight second guessing this visit.

"My bad then."

"So, how's business?" she asked as her maid brought out two glasses of wine.

"Same ole shit I guess," Knight stated.

"Is that right?"

"Why, you heard something?" He could tell she was fishing for something.

"The Cuban bitches are trying everything to ruin us," she told him.

"They shot open Lil K's wedding in Puerto Rico." Knight was still upset about that.

"I know," she stated.

"What you mean you know?" he asked.

"I have a few spies in the Cuban Cartel circle shill out," MeMe said, knowing what he was thinking.

"That's good to know now, I guess."

"Aliza is in Miami," MeMe said with her legs crossed, enjoying the strong taste of wine.

"Miami?"

"Yeah. They just brought a mover to your ex-plug," MeMe said with a smirk. MeMe didn't really care for Julie, but they never had beef or crossed paths so Julie was good in her book.

"She okay?"

"Yeah, but this will start a big war. The Cuban sisters will have their hands full so it will be a good time to strike," she stated.

"I see your vision, but it could backfire also."

"Only if you let it," she said, looking close at one of her paintings, which was worth $3.8 million.

"You got a plan?"

"No, we play it by ear, but I like the way you move, Knight. You're every drug lord's dream," she said, looking at him.

"Thanks."

"No problem. Have you connected with my sister's boyfriend?" she wanted to know.

"Nah, was I supposed to?"

"No, but it would be much easier to ship both of your loads at the same time because y'all right next to each other." She told him something she'd been thinking.

"That's on you. I don't mind. Whatever will be easy for you," he stated.

"Okay, let me speak to my sister and Wolf to see if they will be cool with it."

"That's fair." Knight stood up, to leave.

"You trying to leave already?" she asked.

"I thought this friendly meeting was over?"

"Yeah, we good, but eat and have a drink with me," she asked.

"I don't mix business with pleasure," he told her in her ear.

"I see you're learning me too well," she said before he left.

Chapter 8
Camaguey, Cuba

Jose Martinez waited for his maids to bring out the wonderful food they'd prepared. The backyard of his mansion was set up like an outdoor restaurant for today's event he was throwing for his family. Today he called a family meeting and only five family members had a seat at the table.

"I'm happy to see everybody here. All my beautiful children - especially my favorites Rachela and Aliza," Jose said, seeing his two sons give each other looks.

Jose's daughters put in much more work in the Martinez Cartel than either of his sons.

"Thanks, Daddy," Rachela said, smiling at her daddy. Growing up, Rachela was a daddy's girl and she still was today.

"We're all here today for the meeting to put some things on the table," Jose stated, taking a sip of water as their food all came out on trays with lids on them.

"What's going on?" Jose's son Colon asked nervously.

"Everybody remove your lids from your trays," Jose said.

When everybody removed their lids, everyone saw food on the trays except Colon. A bloody hand was on his tray with a wedding ring. The cut-off hand looked familiar to him, but he couldn't pinpoint it.

"As you see, everybody has food on their tray except one person," Jose looked at Colon.

"What's this?" Colon was upset, trying to figure out what was going on.

"Your greed," Jose said.

"What do you mean, Father? I've been loyal to you," Colon stated.

"To me?" Jose said.

Rachela took a sip of wine, leaning back and watching the movie take off. She knew what Colon had done. She was the one who told her father about his disloyalty. She wanted to kill him herself but he told her not to because he had it on lock.

"Yes."

"So, you didn't try to turn my men against me to take over my turf out here in Camaguey?" Jose asked.

Colon looked at the hand on tray and knew who it was: his beautiful wife.   "You killed my wife?"

"You killed your wife, Colon," Jose said, now pulling out a gun.

"I done nothing!" he yelled in tears.

"Colon, the gag is up. We caught you," Rachela said.

"Fuck you, slut!" Colon yelled.

"Fine." Rachela shrugged her little shoulders.

"We don't need people like you in our circle." Jose aimed his gun at his own son, standing up.

Boc! Boc! Boc! Boc! Boc! Boc! Boc!

Rachela started clapping as Aliza shook her head.

"Now that's done, we have a bigger problem at hand, and that's the States. What's the update on Julie?" Jose asked, eating dinner.

"She is hiding out, but I have our people on it," Aliza stated.

"I want her dead," Jose told her.

"I'm on it." Aliza knew what she had to do.

"Rachela, what's the update on this Knight kid?"

"I'm gonna need time. This ain't as easy as Julie. He's down with some serious people," Rachela said.

"I don't give a fuck who he's down with," Jose told her.

Aliza laughed under her breath because Rachela just tried to fix on her.

"I'm working on it," Rachela repeated.

"Work harder." Her father then looked at his other son who was eating.

"I'm still in Brazil, Father. I got everything set up for your mission," Hilton said.

"Sounds good, Son. Now everybody eat up. You gonna need it," Jose told them all.

"What are we going to do about the Costa Rican sisters?" Rachela asked, knowing they were going to be a major issue," she said.

"What do you mean?" Jose asked.

"I need more manpower," she said, making everybody at the table laugh because she never ran into this type of problem.

Everybody knew the Costa Rican sisters' reach was strong.

"I got you, my beautiful daughter. Trust me, you will have all the manpower you'll need," Jose said.

"Thank you."

Romell Tukes

Chapter 9
Manhattan, NY

OG had Maryanna on all fours in the penthouse suite.

"Ohhhh yessss," Maryanna yelled while getting pounded out by her husband.

Maryanna had a nice big round ass and big breasts swinging back and forth while she gripped the hotel sheets.

"Yesss, daddyyyy." Her moans were loud and shaking the wall.

OG was on his last pump before he pulled off her wet tight pussy. This was an every night routine for the lovebirds. They were bonded by their sex and chemistry for years. Nobody knew about their love affair because they were two powerful people when they met. Luckily, OG was able to get outta jail with the help of his girl.

"I'm gonna take a nap before we take our trip," OG stated, laying down.

"I'm gonna take a shower then," she said, going into the bathroom.

Maryanna looked like she could be on *America's Next Top Model* with the body of a stripper. Her Dominican beauty was outstanding. Maryanna was one of the prettiest women that walked the planet and also deadly. Maryanna trained Wolf how to shoot and fight his enemy and she trained him well. She had plans with OG to take over New York City as a whole, but she had to crew before she could walk. Taking over Harlem and Spanish Harlem was an easy task, but her main target was to take over Yonkers and the Bronx.

Wolf had Yonkers on lock and she was upset about that, but the main reason she was mad was because word was that Wolf's connect was the Costa Rican sisters. The Costa Rican sisters hated Maryanna and they killed OG's brother and sister years ago in Cuba.

She put the water on warm and soaked her body, letting it roll off her skin as the shower glass doors slid open.

"I couldn't sit back and watch you take a shower alone, sexy," OG said, creeping up behind her.

"Ummm, I love you, daddy," she said.

"I know."

"I hope you do," she said, turning around, dropping to her knees, taking his manhood in her mouth.

She sucked his cock for over twenty minutes in the shower, making him go crazy.

***

Harlem, NY

On the east side of Harlem, Rocky's name was like Jay Z's to the rap game. Rocky came from Carver Projects, one of the most money-getting spots on the east side. Working for Maryanna and OG wasn't too bad but the ups to doing business with them is they dropped off 100 keys or more every load. Rocky was twenty two years old driving around in luxury cars flexing. His shooters were all from his hood, so they were mainly Crips and Bloods.

"Yo Rocky!" Pee yelled, coming from the store, seeing Rocky get out of his car. Pee was his Uncle who Rocky tried to put on by giving him a pack to get some money, but he smoked it all.

"What the fuck you want, Pee?" Rocky ain't even called him Uncle no more because he lost respect for him when he crossed him.

"I need some money." Pee's face was ashy and dirty.

Back in the day, Pee used to be one of the top dealers in Harlem. His name was heavy. When he caught a ten year bid he came home with a new drug habit. Pee came out smoking crack and sniffing coke, but nobody knew of his habits until it was too late.

"Nigga, your bum ass still owes me $100,000," Rocky said.

"Nephew——"

"Don't call me nephew. You a disgrace, nigga," Rocky told him, making the sexy woman in the car laugh at Pee.

"Fuck you, little nigga! That's why your dad was out here sucking dick for a high before he died of AIDS!" Pee spit, upset his nephew just flexed on him.

Rocky dad was a crackhead who had HIV, but never did shit for his kicks. In a quick motion, Rocky pulled out a gun.

Boc! Boc! Boc!

He shot Pee three times in the stomach.

"Ahhhhhhhh!" Pee screamed like a bitch.

The woman in the car got out and ran up the block. She always heard rumors about how crazy Rocky was.

"Talk that fly shit now, hoe-ass nigga." Rocky stood over his bleeding Uncle.

"I'm sorry."

"Huh?"

"Sorry," Pee moaned, holding on to the holes to stop them from bleeding out more.

"You lucky. I want to kill your crackhead ass," Rocky said to him before walking off.

Rocky had to go meet up with his cousin Manny in Lincoln Projects.

Pee ended up dying at the hospital later but Rocky didn't give a fuck because Pee was worthless in his eyes.

Romell Tukes

Chapter 10
Miami Beach, FL

Julie moved to the nice Miami Beach area to get outta Dade County since her worker was found hanging from her gate. It was war time and she wanted the blood of every Cuban on her hands.

She loved her new home. It was like her last home, but the place looked alluring. Today Knight was coming by for a sit down. She reached out to him this time because she needed his help this time. Julie needed more manpower and Knight had all the reach she needed because he dealt with the Costa Ricans. She now had guards surrounding the house just in case the Cubans tried anything.

"They just pulled up, boss," a baldheaded man in a suit stated, wearing an earpiece.

"Send him in here," Julie said, sitting in her mid-size office.

Seconds later, Knight walked in wearing a nice suit with matching shoes.

"Hey," Julie said, on her best behavior.

"Julie, nice to see you," Knight said, taking a seat.

"How you been?"

"Well."

"I've been hearing good news about you," she said.

"Oh, is that right?"

"Yes."

"Julie, why did you call me? Because when I came out here a few months ago, you shitted on me," he said.

"I'm sorry, I get feisty when I'm on my period," she told him, hoping he believed it.

"What do you want? And cut the shit," Knight told her.

"Okay, I need your help," she admitted.

"Not you, Ms. Julie, the super woman with super powers," he said with a funny expression on his face.

"Stop, Knight."

"What's up?"

"The Cubans," she said.

"What about them?" Knight already knew Julie's problems. He just wanted to hear it from her own mouth.

"They're trying to kill me and I need a hand," Julie said.

"Why should I help?" he asked.

"If not for me, then do it for your family, because they gonna come for him too," Julie made a clear point.

"The Martinez Cartel?" Knight asked her.

"Yes."

"Give me some time to come up with something," he said.

"I may not have time, Knight. These people run Miami underworld and nine times outta ten they'll know I'm here." Julie looked at him, giving him the cry for help look.

"Okay, I understand, and I got you. Wherever I go, I know the Cubans won't be too far behind me," he stated.

"I see where you going with this." She smiled.

"True."

"I'll be waiting on my time. How's Lil K?" she asked.

"He just got married to Khalid's daughter."

"Oh, that assistant chick?" Julie had heard about Behadi.

"Yeah."

"Good, that's great," Julie stated.

"How about your love life?" Knight asked her.

"Dry like a desert," she laughed.

"I can't believe that shit, ma," Knight shot back.

"You better."

"I just think you too busy and you don't trust anybody with your love," Knight told her.

"Okay, maybe you're Dr. Phil, but what's going on with your love life?" she asked him.

"Single and not looking. I don't have time for drama."

"I'm surprised you not with MeMe, but then again, she may be a little too much for you."

"No woman is too much for me."

"That's the key. MeMe isn't a woman. She is a rare breed. Don't let her looks fool you," Julie told Knight, trying to warn him.

"Did I let your looks fool me?"

"Yes."

"No, I didn't," Knight shot back, remembering when he first met her years ago.

"Okay, tell yourself this. But I have to say I'm proud of you because you came a long way," she said seriously.

"I'm glad you noticed."

"I remember you were just a young handsome kid from the Bronx with a diamond grill trying to get on and now you're a kingpin," Julie said.

"Facts."

"Big facts," she added.

"I'm gonna get at you in a few days." Knight got up.

"Please do."

Romell Tukes

Chapter 11
City Island, BX

Lil K noticed Behadi was down today and sad, so he took her to City Island, her favorite seafood spot. Behadi loved seafood so he knew a nice dinner date then out on the town would make her day. She had been a little down since their marriage, especially after her wedding got crashed.

"Why you not eating?" Lil K asked her, knowing she had mood swings.

"I'm great, blessed, happy, all in one." She put on a fake smile but Lil K knew when she was being a smart ass.

"What's really going on, ma? Your energy is off," he stated.

"I'm sorry I'm not the wife you envisioned."

"Behadi, talk."

"Okay, tough guy, I want that bitch who ambushed our wedding."

"I agree."

"So, why you not doing nothing then?" she asked.

"I'm focused on business."

"Dem people almost killed you, your brother and your wife, and you're worried about business."

"Yeah."

"That's weak as hell," she said, not holding shit back.

"We gonna get dem back, trust me."

"I want to get them back now!" Behadi shouted.

"It's not our call," he told her.

"So whose call is it?"

"What the fuck you mean?" Lil K was starting to get frustrated.

"Knight?"

"What about him?"

"It's up to him, I bet," she replied.

"Why does it matter, baby?" He knew what she wanted now. The look was all in her eyes.

"I want to kill them all," Behadi told her.

"How come you ain't say that from the jump? Come on," Lil K said, getting up, leaving in his Islamic garment and kufi.

***

Hollywood, CA

D Fatal Brim and Marie were going back and forth in the bedroom about him opening shop in New Jersey and upstate New York. He had some homies who he was in touch with from New Jersey and upstate NY.

"L.A. isn't enough for you?" she yelled.

"Of course, but you're missing my point," he told her.

"How?"

"Network," he said.

"We're taking over the whole west coast, we even have the Gulf of Mexico. What more can you ask, Fatal?" Marie saw greed in his eyes and she knew that was the quickest way to a downfall.

"I'll be up there for a few months then back," he said.

"Oh hell no!" she yelled in her strong Mexican accent.

"No, what?"

"You not going up there alone," she told him.

"Baby——"

"No, I'm coming with you," she stated, seriously.

"What? You trippin," he said.

"Never. I'm coming, bet that shit," Marie said in her ghetto voice, making him laugh.

"Okay."

"I knew you'd give in, baby," she said, kissing his lips.

"When you gonna be ready to leave?"

"Soon."

"What's soon, Marie?" D Fatal Brim knew her soon could add up to months.

"A few weeks. I have to go visit a cartel family first, then we can go up north," she asked.

"Okay, are you sure?"

"Yes, papi. Now can we go have make up sex? I want you to bang out my ass tonight, okay?" she demanded.

"Sure, let's get it started, nasty."

"You nasty, daddy, and I love every bit of it," she replied.

Romell Tukes

Chapter 12
Costa Rica, San Jose

Jose Martinez's wife, Oannai, was on a three day vacation in Costa Rica with a man she'd been having an affair with. Oannai had been cheating on Jose for years, mainly with black men who treated her well. She was in an expensive resort laid up and the strong scent of sex musk could be smelled.

"That was amazing, but I'm hungry," she told the young and handsome black man.

"Word, but go cook," he said.

"How about we order food? Because I can't cook," she said.

"What are you good for?"

"Sucking dick and fucking," she blurted out.

"You right about that, baby. Too bad your old man can't keep up with that good pussy," he said.

"Yep, but you can." She rubbed on his massive cock, about to go down on him, until a gang of gunmen ran into the room.

Boc! Boc! Boc! Boc! Boc! Boc! Boc!

The gunmen killed her boyfriend as she covered her mouth, scared to death.

"You a bad girl." A woman walked into the room in heels and a sexy two-piece dress.

The woman was MeMe and she wasn't here to play games, Oannai could tell.

"Please don't."

"Don't what?"

"Kill me."

"That's a really dumb thing to say. Look beside you. Now what do you think the chances are that you go back to Cuba to Jose?" MeMe asked.

"I'll do anything."

"Okay."

"I'll tell you where Jesus is buried, anything," Oannai begged for her life.

"Where is Jose?" MeMe asked as a funny smirk popped up on her face.

"Bitch, I'm gonna die anyway, fuck you." Oannai laughed out loud like the Joker because she knew she had her going.

"Good one." MeMe had to give it to her.

Boc! Boc! Boc! Boc! Boc! Boc! Boc! Boc!

Seeing Oannai was dead for sure, she left the nice resort she owned. The resort had been in her family for years over a hundred years and counting but it was passed down to her.

MeMe and her sister owned six other beautiful resorts so they not only were two of the biggest drug suppliers, but they owned hotels also.

MeMe made her way home to meet with her sister and other family members to enjoy a dinner.

Chapter 13
Yonkers, NY

Wolf had a nice two-story home in the suburbs of Yonkers, NY. He came home to his birth place and the place that helped him become who he was now. His child was in the back room asleep. Having a baby girl with Keiline, a queenpin, wasn't easy because they both lived a busy life. Right now Keiline was in Costa Rica chilling and handling business affairs for them.

The thing Keiline liked about Wolf is that he was a good dad. Parenting for both of them was easy. They understood each other's ways of raising a child and how they were both raised. Wolf had never met a woman like her before. She also supplied his mother Rita back in the day so she knew of him.

Being back in Yonkers felt like being at home rather than being in Costa Rica, a land he could never get used to. The beef with the Cubans was going to get outta hand sooner or later. Wolf knew his girl and MeMe had a big enough army to go to war with the Cubans and win any day. Wolf had to focus on his Yonkers crew moving shit all through Westchester County and all the way up to Buffalo. Shit in Yonkers was a lot different since he left, but he knew money and drugs will forever run the city.

Tomorrow he was supposed to meet with his crew to discuss product and numbers.

***

South Bronx, NY

J Balla had to go pick up his son from school and take him to his crazy-ass baby mother's crib. His baby mother was a sexy Puerto Rican woman, but she was very crazy. Having two kids by two different Puerto Rican women was more than a headache. After he dropped off his son, he had to go meet his little homie SK Balla.

His cousin SK Balla just came home from an up north bid from a robbery and gun charge. J Balla just wanted to roll out the red carpet for him and show him love.

When he rolled up to the school, his son was already outside with other kids. J Balla was never on time when it came to picking up Lil James so he knew he was on point.

"What's up, little man?" J Balla got out of his car and helped his son take off his book bag and place it in the back.

"Hi Dad," Lil James replied in a dead tone.

"Damn, you had a bad day or something, little nigga?" J Balla looked at his handsome son, who had colorful eyes and curly hair.

"Mommy said not to use that word," said Lil James.

"What word?"

"The N word."

"Mommy not here now, is she?" J Balla shouted back.

"No."

"Okay then. How was school today, and what did you do?"

"Ummm, a lot of reading and math." Lil James got good grades, all A's and B's. Every time he did well in school, J Balla would buy him a video game or pair of shoes to reward him.

"I'm proud of you."

"Can I ask you something, Daddy?" Lil James asked.

"Anything, little man."

"Are you a bad guy?" he asked as J Balla drove through the busy streets.

"Bad guy?"

"Yeah, you know, like the cops and robbers."

"Who told you that?"

"I overheard Mommy talking about you."

"To who?" J Balla was a little upset.

"Grandma, in Spanish."

"I'm not perfect, but I'm a good guy who has made some mistakes."

"Okay." Lil James nodded.

"In life, we all gonna make mistakes, but it takes a bigger man to better himself," J Balla told his son, pulling up to his baby mother's house.

J Balla saw his baby mother looking out the window as he stayed in the car.

"I love you, Dad."

"Love you more," J Balla told him, watching his son walk up in the crib he bought and paid for.

J Balla didn't fuck with none of his baby mothers because when he went to jail, they left him for dead, thinking he was gonna blow trial and never come home. When he came home, they tried to act like nothing happened, but he couldn't deal with the fake and they were both fake. He still took care of his kids.

***

Uptown, Bronx

J Balla took SK Balla and a few other niggas out to a club that night. SK Balla got so drunk he threw up in the V.I.P. section and all over some dark-skinned bitch there having a good time. The club was turned up. The Bronx was in the building and J Balla got wild love from everybody there. Later that night, the homies had to take SK Balla home because he couldn't even walk. J Balla had a blast laughing at his boy.

Romell Tukes

Chapter 14
Newark, NJ

Rachela took a private jet to New Jersey to her home she'd be staying at while she kept a close eye on the city next door. She knew Knight was in the Bronx so she planned to keep tabs on him and destroy whatever she could. She carried ten goons with her from Cuba; they were ready for war at all times. The news of her dad's wife's death made her laugh because she disliked her.

Jose Martinez was crushed over his wife's death even though he knew she was having an affair with someone. Going to Costa Rica to cheat was the dumbest shit Rachela thought the bitch could do because everybody knew about the beef with them and the Costa Rican sisters.

The flight landed and Rachela was tired. She hadn't slept in days because she had been moving around daily. She wore a red Dolce and Gabbana dress and six inch heels, looking like a sexy devil. Her guards made their way off the plane first at the Newark Airport. Rachela got into her awaiting SUV and drove off towards the highway. There were three trucks with her and she was in the second one, on her way to the condo on the border line of New Jersey and New York.

She heard a motorcycle pulling up on the SUV. There was tint on the windows because she liked to be low-key. She realized there was a woman on the bike, which she never saw in her country. When Rachela saw the woman take off the helmet and toss it on the ground, she yelled for the driver to run the red light.

Behadi read her lips and opened fire on all three SUV's with a Draco.

Tat! Tat! Tat! Tat! Tat! Tat! Tat! Tat! Tat! Tat! Tat! Tat!

Behadi killed everybody in the first and third SUV, but Rachela's driver sped into the opposite lane, getting away from the bullets. Rachela's heartbeat was going crazy nonstop. She had no clue how Behadi got to her so quickly, but she remembered something odd about one of her guards. On the flight, one of her guards was asking a lot of questions and doing a lot of texting.

"Neal?"

"Yes?"

Neal was Spanish. He worked for Rachela, but he also had ties to the Bronx where his family was from.

"Can I use your phone?" she asked.

"Huh?" Neal turned around from the passenger seat with sweat on his forehead.

"Let me see your phone. My battery is dead. Do I need to say it in Spanish?"

"Here you go, boss." He handed her the phone.

Rachela quickly went through his sent texts and saw these messages:

"In ten minutes," Neal texted.

"Are you sure," Behadi responded.

"Yes we will be outside of the airport in three SUV's. Rachela always rides in the second one. I need my $100,000," Neal texted.

"Okay we will take care of you." Behadi's last response.

"You," Rachela said, pulling out her gun and shooting Neal in the back of the head, killing him.

She knew there was something funny about him and now she had proof.

Chapter 15
Bronx, NY

Knight couldn't believe MeMe called him telling him she was in the city at her new condo she just got last week. Lil K told him about how one of Rachela's workers was cool with his boy Ralph. The man's name was Neal and he was able to blackmail him into turning on Rachela.

Ned gave up Rachela's location so Lil K was able to form a plan, but he had no idea Behadi would beat him to the punch. Behadi paid Ned an extra $100,000 to get Rachela there earlier before Lil K got a hold of her. She wanted Rachela's blood for fucking up her wedding that day by trying to kill them. When Lil K told him about this he was surprised at how hard Behadi was on Rachela's ass.

Knight drove all the way to the city listening to some old school DMX.

***

Manhattan, NY

MeMe loved the sight of the beautiful city they called the rotten apple and the city of dreams. She came to New York to get away from her homeland and to check on Knight. The condo she bought had two levels. It was a masterpiece and she planned to be here more. Her sister was also in and out of Yonkers with Wolf but she also had dealings in Miami. Knight was on her camera monitors outside. MeMe had personal guards down stairs in the lobby with the security guards who worked there.

"MeMe," Knight said, opening the door.

"Come inside," she yelled, pouring two glasses of wine.

"Wow."

"What?" she said.

"This place is ode fire," Knight said.

"Odee fire?" she replied, confused with the way he talked. MeMe didn't understand half the shit Knight said half the time but she thought it was cute.

"It's nice."

"Oh yeah, of course. I have to have the best but when you're going to show me around the city." She approached him, handing him a glass of red wine.

"I ain't know you pulled up," he told her.

"You know now."

"I got you."

"We killed Jose's wife, but I'm sure he's going to try to come back ten times harder," MeMe stated, sitting down.

"Fuck him."

"I agree."

"Behadi almost killed Rachela the other day," Knight said.

"That girl got skills. I swear you're lucky to have her," MeMe said, sipping her wine.

"Rachela managed to escape the whole thing without a scratch on that bitch."

"Behadi went to Cuba?"

"No."

"I don't understand how she was able to get close to her?" MeMe had to know.

"Rachela came out to New Jersey," Knight told her.

"She what?"

"In Jersey, next door."

"That bitch!" MeMe knew Jose would try to send one of his daughter's out here to handle his work."

"This is good."

"You think?"

"Yes."

"Why?" she asked.

"She is on my turf now. Whether it's Jersey or New York, me and Lil K have connections all over the east coast," he said.

"We have to stay on ours too, but I'm gonna stay out here for a while," MeMe said.

"You sure?"

"Yes, why not? You don't want me in your city?" she asked.

"I don't care, but this is the BX, not Costa Rica. Shit a little different out here, mami."

"Fine. I don't mind," she said, feeling tipsy.

"Okay."

"Why you single? You're very sexy, Knight," MeMe said.

Knight paused because this was the first time she came on to him. Staring at her fat cameltoe and perfect breasts sitting up, nicely he had to control his hardened manhood.

"I haven't found the right one maybe," he said as she got closer.

"Maybe you haven't looked in the right place," she said sexually in a low-pitched voice.

"I'm gonna go, MeMe. I'll call you tomorrow," he said, getting up to leave, feeling hot.

"You don't have to leave, Knight, if you don't want to. I have five private rooms," she told him.

"I'm good. I have to go check on something." He got the fuck up outta there, walking to the door.

Knight knew she was drunk and he didn't want to take advantage of her, even though she was one of the baddest bitches he ever laid eyes on.

"Knight," she called out before he made it out.

"Yo?"

"Thanks," she said.

"Thanks for what?" He was confused.

"I wasn't drunk."

"Huh."

"It's non-alcohol wine," she said back.

"That was a test?" he asked, looking at her grin.

"Life is a test."

"I see."

"Tomorrow you're taking me to breakfast on a date," MeMe told him.

"How about a business date," he corrected her, turning her down.

"Oh, okay, cool." She sounded sad. She'd never been turned down. She heard the door close and was upset Knight just denied her, but it made her now want him more for some reason.

Chapter 16
Cuba

Jose Martinez went on a fishing trip with another Cuban Cartel boss.

"It's a nice day today," Jose said, fishing with sunglasses on.

"I agree," Zaleodon said.

"How's life treating you and your family?" Jose asked.

"Great! I just bought twenty acres of land for my horses and cattle," Zaleodon said, hoping to catch some fish.

"Good. I've been busy dealing with the Costa Rican sister bitches," Jose said.

"I never knew you had problems with them?"

"Yeah, it's getting worse day by day," Jose said.

"Damn, I wish I could be of some help." Zaleodon saw Jose put his fishing rod down.

"They killed my wife." Jose's voice got cold.

"I'm sorry to hear that, Jose, really."

"I am too." Jose pulled out a gold pistol with an extended gold clip hanging.

"What's this about, Jose? I done nothing," the Cuban boss said nervously. Zaleodon knew there was something funny about Jose calling him out to go fishing. The two men never saw eye to eye so when Jose tried to call for a truce, he thought it was odd.

"You deal with the Costa Rican sisters. I'm not dumb," Jose said.

"I used to."

"I know better than to believe that shit." Jose laughed out loud.

"I can help you."

"Help me?"

"Yes. I can help you take them down," Zaleodon said..

"I can't trust you," Jose told him before pulling the trigger on him.

Bloc! Bloc! Bloc! Bloc! Bloc! Bloc! Bloc! Bloc! Bloc!

Zaleodon's body fell on the upper deck onto the sidewalk way off the boat. Jose went back to his peaceful fishing. The death of his wife sparked the light in the old Jose.

***

Mexico City, Mexico

Marie went to pay a visit to the Mena Cartel, who had a big portion of Mexico City where they were from. Three trucks entered the gated mansion surrounded by guards with weapons. Marie came with a few men. She always traveled with a few shooters. Things were going so good back home in L.A. thanks to D Fatal Brim having ties to almost every black gang in the city. Going to NY was only trouble but she knew D Fatal Brim had a plan and being his wife she had no choice but to be down with him.

A beautiful woman with golden skin walked outside, opening the door for her.

"Marie, you look so beautiful I swear," LaMena said with a nice silk dress on.

"So do you."

"Thanks, I try. Come in. You're right on time for lunch," La Mena said, walking through her lush home worth millions.

"It's beautiful here." Marie liked her expensive taste.

"Thank you." LaMena sat down at her dinner table ready to eat.

Marie and LaMena both shared the same pipelines to traffic drugs from Mexico to Texas with their workers. The two also did good business together and their families before them did business together, so they kept that torch lit.

"This month is going to be very busy," LaMena said.

"Yes."

"I wanted to speak to you about us opening another tunnel."

"Where?" Marie asked, thinking one pipeline was enough.

"Texas, on the Gulf line," LaMena said.

"That's going to be hard."

"Why you say that?" LaMena asked.

"We have to speak to the cartel who runs that area," Marie said.

"The Diaz Cartel?" LaMena got up.

"Yeah."

"Come with me out back real quick," LaMena said, walking back out.

Once in a small guest house, Marie saw a group of men watch two mountain lions circle around an older man who Marie had seen before.

"That's the Diaz Cartel's boss now. All we gotta worry about is his son Lil Diaz," LaMena smiled.

"This can be bad," Marie said, knowing the border could get nasty for her people if this shit back fired.

"All good. But shall we finish lunch?"

"Sure."

Back at the table, lunch was served hot and spicy as they both loved their Mexican food.

"Do you know a Julie from Miami?" LaMena asked.

"Yeah, somewhat."

"She is good people and I want you to get in contact with her."

"Me? Why?" Marie asked.

"I believe you can use a person like her and she will be a part of this new pipeline," LaMena said.

"How many people do you plan on letting into this new pipeline, LaMena?"

"Just us three, okay? Julie is very loyal."

"Loyalty is rare in this field."

"I know, but she is a big part of this new operation. Trust me, it will be very helpful to us both," LaMena was serious.

"I believe you."

"Okay, now let's eat. I'm very hungry and I have a day of fun planned for us," LaMena said, drinking a glass of cold ice water.

Romell Tukes

Chapter 17
Bronx, NY

Behadi grabbed the back of both ankles while Lil K fucked her doggy style, spreading her soft ass cheeks apart.

"Ugghhh, yesss, babyyy!" she yelled as they went from making love in the living room to fucking in the bedroom.

Lil K loved the way her wetness and sex muscles squeezed his manhood.

"Shittt, oh my God!" she screamed, feeling her climax about to reach its boiling point.

"You love it when I fuck you like this, don't you?" Lil K said, sliding in and out of her seeing her juices all over his rod.

"Yesss, I'm cumming, keep fucking me, daddy, shit!" she cried out loud, closing her eyes, taking every inch of him.

Behadi came and she let him pull out, but little did he know she had other plans. She took his dick and shoved it in the back of her throat, going as deep as she could the first try. She sucked slowly, going up, Lil K loved the sensual feeling she was putting on him.

"Damn, girl," he said, seeing her head go up and down as she worked her lips and tongue.

It only took a few minutes for him to nut and she caught all of it.

"Don't get used to me swallowing all that," she said.

"I won't."

"I want to watch a movie, baby."

"Okay. I'm down, what we watching? I'm going to get some wine."

"*New Jack City*," she stated, excited.

"You sure, baby?" Lil K asked because he had watched that movie with her over a thousand times.

"I'm sure. Why, you wanna watch *Belly*?" she asked.

"No."

"*Belly 2*?" she asked again, knowing his favorite movie was *Belly* with Nas and the late DMX.

"*New Jack City* cool, I guess," Lil K said, seeing a call from J Balla come in on his phone.

"A'ight."

"J Balla got an issue in MillBrook," Lil K said.

"MillBrook? Ain't that your hood?" she asked, knowing he was from there.

"Yeah. I have to go ma." He started to get dressed, thinking the worst.

Lil K knew the crew had beef with the Cubans and he knew from dealing with the last Cubans that their reach was long.

"Want me to come?" Behadi got outta bed ass naked, showing her sexy body.

"Nah, I'll be right back, you heard?" he said, leaving her upset.

***

MillBrook, Bronx

The projects had yellow tape all around it and NYPD cop cars and EMS trucks all over the place. MillBrook projects was one of Lil K's main money-getting turfs and everybody knew this. Nine people had been shot and killed and seven seriously wounded including a little toddler. Lil K saw J Balla across the street with a few people pissed off.

"Niggas slid on the hood."

"I see. It looks like a fucking school shooting out here," Lil K looked at all the lights surrounding the place.

"This nigga was pulling up into the projects when he saw the shit going down," J Balla said, looking at his homie Jet Boy.

"Shit was ill, son, word to me," Jet Boy said.

"What happened?"

"I saw a gang of tatted-up Mexicans jump out of trucks and start spraying. I can't cap; I got low, bro. I'm not trying to get hit," Jet Boy said.

"Did you see amigos?" Lil K asked.

"The MS-13 kind, but I also saw the hat boy who used to be out here," Jet Boy said, trying to think of dude's name.

"Hat boy?" Lil Ki was confused as to who he was talking about.

"The Blood nigga who used to be out here turned up on everybody," Jet Boy said.

"You don't know the boy's name, son?" J Balla asked.

"Brim or some shit," Jet Boy tried to remember.

"Brim? I know a lot of Brims," J Balla stated.

"Hold on. D Fatal Brim?" Lil K asked.

"Yeah, him, bro. He was the main nigga killing shit," Jet Boy told them.

"I can't believe this," Lil K said.

"You better," J Balla said, knowing who D Fatal Brim was also.

Romell Tukes

Chapter 18
Yonkers, NY

Chills and TT both waited for their drug connect to show up at a low-key sneaker store. Both of the men were big hitters in Yonkers, both from different sides of the town. Chills was from a street they called O-Block and TT came from School Street projects, one of the worst projects in the city.

"This nigga on a private jet to us?" TT joked.

"You got no patience, bro." Chills stood out front of his store smoking a cigarette.

"I do, but what the fuck, son? I'm tired as hell. Last night was one hell of a night in Jersey," TT said, thinking about his big 25th birthday party he had in Jersey City.

"That shit was popping, brody, I can't lie. Shit was sturdy, bro. You did that, son," Chills said, thinking back to last night.

"I know, nigga. I saw you leave with two bitches," TT said, seeing a Bentley pull up.

"There he go," Chills said as Wolf got out of the luxury car.

"Yeroooo," Wolf shouted.

"Yo, what da vibes?" Chills said, chain hanging and watch blinging.

"Wolf, what's really good?" TT embraced the man who had put him and Chills on to a big bag.

"I'm gonna be back for a while. I plan to stick around. I know in my last meeting I told y'all I wasn't but I think I'm gonna stick around," Wolf told them.

"Cool. I'm for that," Chills said.

"Word," TT added.

"I want to expand though," Wolf said.

"To where?" TT asked, because they already had Yonkers on lock.

"The city," Wolf said.

"The Bronx is already under control of a nigga named J Balla or some shit," Chills said.

"We fucks with the Bronx, son, facts, but I was thinking more like Harlem or some shit," Wolf said.

"Oh," TT said.

"I got some people out there too." Chill's older brother was doing big things out there.

"We litty then," Wolf said, looking at all the traffic going into the shop.

"I need some more work when you get good," Chills said.

"Got you. Give me a day or two," Wolf said before walking back to his car.

***

Riverdale, Yonkers

Wolf pulled into a local gas station to fill up his tank real quick. Dealing with Chills and TT was easy. They were good loyal workers. He had met both men a few years back in Miami at a strip club and it'd been litty ever since. Opening shop in Harlem would be a fight, but he needed to expand. Yonkers was enough because Westchester County was small but the city wasn't.

He went to pay for gas and grab a bottle of soda. He planned to go home and take a nap before his baby mother arrived. Walking outside, he saw a sexy Spanish woman leaning on his car as if she lost her mind.

"You good, ma?" Wolf said as he got closer.

"Yep."

"Why you on my shit?" Wolf said, getting a good look at her to see she was his auntie he hasn't seen in a while.

"Hey Wolf."

"Auntie Maryanna, where you been?" he asked.

"Busy," she said.

Wolf couldn't believe how good and youthful she still looked right now. "Why are you here?" Wolf wasn't dumb.

"You really don't know?" she asked.

"No, I don't." Wolf knew his auntie played mind games.

"Your brother's father."

"OG?"

"Yes," Maryanna said, looking into his eyes.

"What about him?"

"I helped him escape from prison a while back, but me and him been together since before your mom," she explained.

"Get to the point."

"OG is a very connected man and we want you on our team. We need you," she said.

"Me?"

"Yes."

"No, I'm good," he said, pumping his gas.

"Okay, this is our last time offering you a spot," she said.

"Fuck you and your offer," he said.

"I'll see you around." She disappeared.

Romell Tukes

Chapter 19
Manhattan, NY

Knight took Lil K out to a nice restaurant to talk and enjoy a nice classy dinner in an upscale restaurant. Lil K hadn't been able to tell his brother about what J Balla told him about D Fatal Brim popping back up. What Lil K didn't understand was why D Fatal Brim wouldn't reach out to Knight, his best friend. Knight was the reason he was even home on his appeal from the jump.

"Why you look stressed out, son? You living the life of a real boss," Knight said.

"It costs to be a boss," Lil K said.

"We paying our dues, bro."

"Facts."

"What's been going on? I know you ain't call me on Kazzy's birthday to have a drink." Knight reminded himself today was his late brother's birthday.

"As Kazzy would say, his C-day." Lil K laughed.

"Yeah, he was one in a million, son. I always knew he was going to be a heavy Crip when he used to watch all them Snoop Dogg videos," Knight joked, thinking back to when they were kids.

"I was a baby then," Lil K said.

"Word, son, but what's really up, bro?" Knight asked. "Oh yeah, where my nigga at?" Knight hoped his boy was around.

"It's not that vibe," Lil K let him know.

"What you mean?"

"He killed our men," Lil K said.

Knight frowned as if he didn't believe a word Lil K just said. "What are you talking about, Lil K?"

"That shit that went down the other day in Millbrook?"

"Yeah."

"That was D Fatal Brim."

Knight had to make sure he wasn't hearing shit.

"Yes. J Balla's little homie saw the whole scene unfold," Lil K stated.

"Fuck, son."

"I was shocked."

"This can't be."

"What is he trying to do, bro?"

"First we have to make sure it's him," Knight said.

"Trust me, it's him."

"I hope not."

"If it is, you know we have to go to war," Lil K said.

"I know, Lil K, but until that time comes, stand down and let's focus on this money."

"A'ight, dawg." Lil K didn't say anything else about it.

***

New York City, NY

Keiline walked through Times Square, sightseeing alone and doing a little shopping here and there at fancy stores. She liked New York. It was so different and busy. People were always on the move and speeding past someone, but she hated the jam-packed traffic while driving through the city areas like Manhattan. Wolf normally showed her around, but he was upstate somewhere. She liked Yonkers. It was nice and quiet. The main thing she loved was all the shopping stores.

They got a babysitter for their daughter so they could move around when needed. Wolf was the best dad. She was glad to have him and she knew he was glad to have a bad boss bitch like her in his corner ride or die.

Chapter 20
Harlem, NY

"Rocky, it wasn't my fault, I swear, bro! I put the brick where you told me to and when I came back the next day, it was all gone," C-Note said, standing in the back parking lot of his complex building on the east side.

C-Note worked for Rocky. The two men grew up together since the sandbox. C-Note got drugs from Rocky on consignment and when he was done with the drugs, he would normally pay Rocky. One thing he didn't know was C-Note and his Uncle TJ had been stealing and getting high together for a few weeks now.

"Who took it?" Rocky asked with two men behind him.

"What you mean? It was your uncle. He was the only one who knew where the stash spot was," C-Note said.

"It was all him?" Rocky gave C-Note a look letting him know he was bull shitting. "I would never cross you Rocky, you family. I-I-I——" C-Note's words began to fumble.

Rocky pulled out a gun and placed it to his childhood friend's head.

"Where my shit?" Rocky asked with fire in his eyes.

"Okay, please don't shoot, I'll tell you everything."

"Talk, nigga. You better hurry," Rocky said, looking at his watch.

"A nigga and his crew pulled up on me and your uncle, offering us money to rob you and to come work for him," C-Note cried out.

Rocky's mind started to spin because the shit ain't sound right to him. "How much?" Rocky had to know how much the double cross was.

"A lot, bro. I swear the dude must have been rich because he was willing to up the price," C-Note said, feeling bad now for trying to cross Rocky since he got caught up. The idea was really his Uncle TJ's. He wasted no time in taking the deal.

"My uncle TJ was down, huh? After all I did for him?" Rocky asked himself.

"Yeah."

"Who was the dude, son? And don't play no game, C-Note, I'll kill your whole family." Rocky's face said it all. He meant business.

"He from Yonkers. They call him Wolf," C-Note said as Rocky looked at his goons as if the name was a joke.

"Wolf?"

"Yeah. A young nigga with a bag. He said something about a nigga named OG and Maryanna," C-Note said.

When Rocky heard OG's and Maryanna's names, he knew whoever Wolf was, he knew Rocky's connect, so this shit could be deeper than him.

"What else he said?" Rocky asked.

"That's it, bro, I swear. I'm sorry." C-Note got teary-eyed, hoping Rocky would have mercy.

"A'ight, go home."

"Okay." C-Note backed up slowly and turned to walk off.

"Yo, C!" yelled Rocky.

"Yeah?" C-Note turned around as he stopped.

Bloc! Bloc! Bloc! Bloc!

Bullets landed in C-Note's face, killing him. Rocky and his goons walked to his SUV parked a few feet away.

"Take me to uptown," Rocky told his driver, thinking about the uncle who raised him, but had now betrayed him.

***

Uptown, Harlem

Uncle TJ was Rocky's blood uncle and the nigga who had showed him the game. He took a big chance by crossing Rocky, but for a half million dollars, he would cross Jesus on a Sunday. Not too many people knew he had a coke habit except his partner in crime C-Note. TJ had plans to cross C-Note when he got his $500,000. He had it all figured out and couldn't wait to be sitting on a mill. He knew eventually Rocky would figure out who robbed him but until then, he would plan his role and stick to the plan he and C-Note came up with. They planned to say some rivals robbed the spot.

Boom!

Jumping off the couch in his apartment he saw three men rush his apartment.

"Don't move, bitch nigga," Rocky said, aiming his Glock 40 at his uncle.

"Nephew, what da fuck is going on?"

"Nigga, shut up." Rocky slapped him with the gun.

"Ahhhhhh shit!" Uncle TJ cried in pain.

"Who paid you to do it?"

"Do what?"

"Nigga, you got two seconds to spill the beans before I spill your brains," Rocky said.

"Wolf from Yonkers, nephew. That's all I know about the dude. Please, I wasn't in the right state of mind, my nigga," Uncle TJ said as Rocky laughed.

"State of mind, huh? From the looks of it, that ain't stop you from sniffing my coke," Rocky said, looking at the coke on the table.

"That's old," Uncle TF said, looking at the drugs.

Bloc! Bloc! Bloc! Bloc!

Rocky called OG as he left the crib, wondering who da fuck was Wolf.

Romell Tukes

Chapter 21
Havana, Cuba

OG arrived in the beautiful country with the most beautiful woman and land he ever saw in any other country. Today he was meeting with the Cubans main boss, Jose Martinez, at his fabulous home.

Jose Martinez supplied OG and Maryanna with so many drugs they could flood half of the States for a few months. Being half-Cuban, OG knew how Cubans' thought process when it came to doing business so he was always on point and he tried not to miss a peep. The only thing OG disliked about doing business with Jose was that he would get disrespectful at times and he hated that.

Yesterday he got a call from his worker Rocky saying he was robbed by a guy, but he said he didn't want to get into detail over the phone. OG promised him when he got back he would stop by to see what was going on.

Maryanna was in the Dominican Republic so Rocky had no choice but to wait. Pulling up to the home of Jose, goons stopped the car driven by Jose's men to do a car check before entering the beautiful real estate.

***

"Your guest is here, Jose," Silent said looking out of Jose's office window.

Silent was Jose's personal killer, his shooter. Jose had known him since he was a kid. He took him off the streets and taught him a new way of living.

"He's early," Jose said, smoking a cigar in a nice custom-fitted suit..

"I don't like him."

"You like money?" Jose said.

"All money not good money," Silent said.

"That's a lie. Money is money, so it can never be good or bad. It's on the person with the money and how he conducts it," Jose said, digging in his drawer.

"I'm leaving," Silent said.

"Where you going?"

"I have to go to Costa Rica to take care of that situation," Silent said.

"Tell our friends I said hello," Jose said.

"I will," Silent said, leaving to see OG coming in. Silent walked right past OG without saying a word.

"My friend." Jose put on a smile.

"I'm here."

"Good. How's New York treating you?" Jose asked, sounding very concerned even though he didn't care.

"It's great."

"I'm sure."

"I tried to get the Wolf kid to come over to my side, but he refused."

"Maybe you ain't try hard enough," Jose said.

"I did. It's not going to happen."

"Listen to me, fucker, I need the Costa Rican bitch and he is our only chance." Jose got real nasty with him.

OG was about to check him, but he took a deep breath and spoke. "How do you know Wolf is down with them?"

"I know shit."

"I'm gonna try."

"Don't fucking try. Just do it," Jose said.

"He waged war with my people by saying fuck our offer. I sent Mary at him - his own flesh and blood. He may be trying to strike right now," OG said, making a point. When Maryanna told him he didn't take her offer, he knew Wolf wouldn't hesitate to go to war.

"Do what needs to be done."

"I will," OG said.

"Good. How's our Maryanna?"

"Great, in D.R. on business," OG said, hating when Jose asked about his wife.

"I'm counting on you both to do right."

"We do right - always."

"How was that last product I sent?"

"Okay," OG said.

"Okay isn't fair."

"I need no cut on my shit to be real," OG said because the last shit had a little cut on it.

"Cut?"

"Yes."

"That must have been your people, OG."

"Never."

"My people don't cut our product. I take that offensive," Jose said, smirking.

"No disrespect."

"None taken. I'm gonna look into it, my friend."

"Thank you. I'll be waiting on the next round."

"Sure, I got you," Jose assured him.

Romell Tukes

Chapter 22
Cartago, Costa Rica

MeMe and Keiline's grandma lived in a beautiful home on a small farm in Cartago. Alayiha was still beautiful for an older woman, but she was dying. Having a serious kidney and lung condition made her chances very thin of making it past ninety more days. If her daughters or nieces weren't there to take care of her then her home nurse was helping with Alayiha's needs.

It was a nice sunny morning and Alayiha wanted her breakfast in bed hooked up to a few IV machines. She heard a loud thump coming from the kitchen making her look out the room door. Seconds later a man she had never seen walked into her room with a plate of food. Alayiha saw the gun in his hand and she knew something bad was going on. Her husband was the reason why her grandbabies were queen pins and the biggest dealers in Costa Rica.

"Hey, old bitch," the man named Silent said, standing over her frail body.

"Your mama's a bitch," she shot back, surprising him.

"Feisty bitch," Silent said before he aimed his gun at her face. Boc! Boc! Boc! Boc! Boc!

Silent left, hoping to send the sisters a message for them to give up and throw in the towel.

***

Caldera, Costa Rica

Knight had never been to this side of the island, but he loved the beautiful home that sat next to a beach. MeMe was on her way downstairs for their meeting today. He was supposed to arrive tomorrow, but he chose to come early. Shit in the town had been a little weird since he heard about D Fatal Brim coming back. Knight wasn't slow. He knew the game, so it was clear what D Fatal Brim was trying to do. Before he let any nigga take over the Bronx, he would risk his own life. New York was his and he'd been expanding into the Brooklyn hoods and other boroughs.

Guards flooded the house all over. When he heard heels clicking coming down the stairs, he knew MeMe was coming down. MeMe walked into the living room with puffy eyes in a sexy black dress. Her beauty was breathtaking every time Knight saw her.

"I'm sorry I'm late," she said, walking on her marble floors.

"It's straight, ma." Knight saw there was something wrong with her. She wasn't her regular self.

"We gonna have to reschedule this meeting."

"Cool."

"Thank you, Knight." She turned to leave, but his voice stopped her.

"MeMe."

"Yes, Knight?"

"What's going on, ma? You can talk to me, it's not all about money. I'm not on that type of time," he said, grabbing her arm to turn her around so she can face him.

"They just killed my grandma," she said emotionally.

"Who?"

"The Cubans."

"I swear I'm gonna kill them, MeMe. I'm so sorry," he said.

"It's da game, Knight. They did what they supposed to," she said in a Spanish accent.

"I'm here for you."

"Are you really?" she asked as she finally showed her soft side.

"Yes."

"You want to pull up, or you got somewhere to be?" She looked him in his eyes, letting him know she really needed his company tonight.

"I'm here." Knight followed her upstairs, telling the guards to leave the house until the morning.

That whole night Knight stayed with her, comforting her. He could have fucked when she kissed him and went down on him, trying to suck his dick, but he refused. She wanted to show him how much she appreciated him being there for her.

The next day, Keiline flew out to bury their grandma and she was hurt about it.

***

L.A, CA

Marie was getting on a private jet to fly to New York to see what her husband was doing because lately, she had been so busy running around. D Fatal Brim in New York was a bad idea, but she knew he would do it with her or without her. Being a good wife at times can cost and risk a lot she was starting to see.

She got comfortable on her jet and took a nap, dreaming about her man's touch.

Romell Tukes

Chapter 23
Manhattan, NY

Hours later, Marie was on her knees taking her husband's cock in and out of her warm mouth. She sucked slowly on D Fatal Brim's pipe as he stood up on his suite terrace.

"Mmmm," he moaned, feeling the back of her throat.

She went a little faster, twisting her head side to side doing the little tricks she knew would make him cum quick.

"Cum for me, papi," she said, sucking the tip with her lips.

"Oh shit, catch it," he moaned, shooting out a load of thick man juices.

"I swallowed it all. Now fuck me like you miss me," she said, standing up, moving her short dress to the side, showing her clean waxed pretty pussy.

D Fatal Brim stood behind her and entered her wetness. He wasn't surprised at how wet she was because Marie's pussy was always dripping.

"Ugghhh, yesss, babyyy!" Marie held on to the rail while he fucked the life outta her.

Marie loved getting fucked doggy style. D Fatal Brim spread her ass cheeks and slid a thumb in her butthole.

"Ohhh!" She jumped forward, but he pulled her back, pumping his pipe into her deeper, leaving his thumb in her tight asshole.

Her screams were so loud the people downstairs heard her and wondered if she was ok or if they should call the police for her.

They had a lovemaking night, then they talked about his plans for New York. She was down as long as she could feel some more good loving.

***
Yonkers, NY

Chills was in the DMV to fix his license but if he would have known the line was this long, he would have tried another day. It took an hour just to get a number for the DMV workers to call when it's your turn. Finally his number got called and he walked up to window seven, where his number appeared on the digital board.

"I'm here to renew my license," Chills told the heavy set older black woman.

"Do you have your license on you?" she asked.

"Yes." Chills pulled out his permit.

"Sir, this is a permit

"I know what it is, I'm here to renew it.

"I left it outside. Look, can I pay you extra? I'm sort of in a rush," he said, seeing her face frown.

"What type of bitch I look like, little nigga? You better take your stank breath ass outside and go get that," she said rudely.

"You fat triple chin bitch," he said.

"Get out the line, big tooth," she shot back.

"That's why McDonalds got an order of protection on you." Chills had other people who were waiting in the line laughing.

"Next!" she yelled.

"Bitch!" Chills walked out.

He walked outside, pissed off about what took place seconds ago. TT called his phone, but he didn't feel like talking to him at all today because last night TT slammed into his car, fucking his rear end up.

Chills peeped a sexy Spanish bitch with two men coming towards him, walking in between cars. He saw there was something off about the scene, but he wasn't tripping until he heard the gunshots.

Boc! Boc! Boc! Boc! Boc! Boc!

Chills ducked as windows shattered all around him from the gunfire. He fired back, hitting one of the men in his side. Chills got a good look at the sexy woman trying to kill him.

Boc! Boc! Boc! Boc!

Shots came from behind Chills. He thought he got trapped in by his opps but it was his young boy from O-Block, Roy.

Boc! Boc! Boc!

Chills was able to hit the other Spanish male as they took off at the sounds of the police sirens that could be heard. When the woman ran off, Chills saw one of the men barely breathing.

"Bitch nigga, who sent you?" Chill placed his Timb boot on the man's chest.

"Please," the man said, coughing out blood.

"Who was that bitch?"

"Maryanna and OG sent us, and they gonna keep coming at y'all," the man said as he died on the spot.

Roy heard the policy getting closer.

"We have to go." Roy grabbed Chills' arms and they left the parking lot.

Chills went to his block thinking about the name the dude told him. Chills knew there was only one person who could make sense out of this and that was Wolf.

Romell Tukes

Chapter 24
South Bronx, NY

SK Balla came outside dripping in a Fendi top and Louis Vuitton skinny jeans with Louis Vuitton sneakers on. Castle Hill projects was litty today. It was a nice day out and the block huggers were scattered all over the projects.

"Hey SK?" a sexy dark-skinned woman with a nice slim frame said as she approached.

SK had been trying to holla at Ayrana for years, but she always gave him the cold shoulder. Everybody knew SK Balla had a thing for dark-skinned women. That was his soft spot.

"What's the vibes, Ayrana," he replied, looking at her C-cup titties sitting nicely in her bra.

"You tell me," she said, smiling, looking at his chain shine when the sunlight caught it.

"I'm straight out here living, ma."

"Oh yeah, I see, but when can you make time for me?" she said, playing with her long hair.

"You still bartending?"

"Yeah."

"I'm gonna pull up to where you be at and catch a vibe with you," he said.

"Say that," she said, walking off to a group of girls waiting for her to hear the gossip. They wanted SK Balla just to get close to J Balla.

Life was good. SK remembered sitting on Riker's Island in a cell wishing one day he would become a boss-type nigga. Thanks to J Balla, he was really out here living his dreams and goals. J Balla was with Lil K, so he figured in a few days the next shipment would be ready because providing the whole Bronx with drugs wasn't easy unless one had an island filled with unlimited coke. Normally as soon as SK Balla got his pack, within days, sometimes hours, it would be all gone.

***

Brooklyn, NY

Lil K and J Balla had just left Flatbush after speaking to one of the head Crips niggas on Church Avenue about supplying him and his section and it turned out well.

"This shit gonna be a good look, son," Lil K said.

"I think so."

"When we getting Staten Island shit locked down?" Lil K asked J Balla, who had his cousin Kash Brim out there.

"I'm waiting for Kash Brim to hit me back with the details, bro."

"Say that, bro." Lil K saw a little Jamaican food spot on the corner and pulled over, making sure the SUV next to him with tint didn't scratch his Audi.

"When you think the product gonna be ready?" J Balla asked as Lil K watched the driver of the white Benz G Wagon try to park but couldn't

"Soon. But yo, this nigga about to hit my shit," Lil K blow his horn.

Lil K and the driver of the SUV hopped out to confront each other.

"I'm sorry. It's hard to park this." The beautiful woman's words stopped when she saw who it was.

Lil K couldn't believe who it was looking sexy in all a white dress. Rachela reached in her car for her gun and so did Lil K, who had his gun under his seat. J Balla saw Lil K's movement and followed Lil K's lead. Nobody saw the police car pulling down the block just driving around.

Bloc! Bloc! Bloc!

Rachela let off the first few shots, hitting Lil K's car, not him, then the police slammed into Lil K's car, making J Balla hit the police car with bullets. Lil K and J Balla ran up the block as Rachela got in her SUV racing off.

The NYPD cop couldn't even chase anybody because he got hit in the neck and died before help could get there.

Blocks away, Lil K and J Balla met in an alley behind two stores.

"Toss these shits," Lil K said as he tossed his gun in the green rusty dumpster.

"Fuck, I think I killed a cop." J Balla cleaned off his pistol with his designer shirt before he threw it in the dumpster.

"That bitch out here trying to take us out. What she doing in Brooklyn?" Lil K asked himself.

"Nigga, did you hear what I said? I just killed a cop," J Balla said seriously, walking out of the alley to see NYPD cop cars zooming past them bumper to bumper.

"You'll be fine. We got bigger problems, son," Lil K said, catching a cab so they could catch a ride to the nearest subway to head back to the BX.

Romell Tukes

Chapter 25
Westchester County, NY

Wolf had a low-key stash house on the outskirts of Yonkers in a decent neighborhood. Chills and TT sat at the small round table surrounded by all white square bricks.

"What we doing, son?" Wolf asked TT as he came out of the kitchen with a bottle of Dom P he sipped on earlier.

"We waiting on you. Our men are one call away," Chills said, leaning back in his chair.

"A'ight, cool. This shit is all y'all," Wolf pointed at the table.

"You ain't even pick up the last re-up money," TT said.

"Don't worry about that. We got something big going on out here and I just want y'all to be on point out here," Wolf said.

"You talkin bout dem Harlem cats?" TT asked.

"It's a little deeper than that son," said Wolf, sitting down.

"Don't you think it would be smart to put us on game, my G," Chills said, looking at Wolf.

"The Spanish bitch is my auntie and she wants us to join here] empire or whatever she got going on." Wolf saw the awkward looks.

"So that bad bitch your auntie?" TT couldn't believe it.

"Yeah, and the nigga she with is my dead brother CB's pops who I killed."

"Hold on, you killed your own brother and now your bro's pops is out to kill you?" TT asked, trying to make sense of it all.

"If you put it like that, cool," Wolf said, shrugging his shoulders, taking a sip of his champagne.

"That's light work, son. We can kill them and that Harlem nigga Rocky and take over Harlem's drug operations," Chills said as if he had come up with the best idea ever.

"It's not as easy as it sounds, playboy, word to life," Wolf told them, standing up.

"So what we gonna do?" TT wanted to know.

"I just hollered at Knight, my son from da BX, and it seems we may have another problem on our hands," Wolf admitted.

"More money, more problems," TT said.

"Facts," Chills added.

"Let me figure this shit out and get back at ya. I gotta go to Miami," Wolf stated.

"Are you about to slide to da 305?" TT asked.

"For a few days," Wolf said, grabbing his car keys.

"A'ight, hit us when you get back," Chills said, ready to get to the bag.

***

Miami, FL

Since losing her grandma, Keiline had been focusing on keeping her mental on an up and up level. That's why she needed to come to Miami - to get a little break from New York. She could have gone back home to Costa Rica, but just thinking about home made her think about her grandma. Wolf came out with her and he was always good company and caring. Keiline had never met a man like Wolf. He knew when to do things and when not to. It was like he was the perfect gentleman to her and she loved that about him.

"You got me." Wolf came up behind her on the beach with two drinks in coconuts.

Miami Beach was lit today with beautiful women showing skin.

"I'm straight, bae," she said, noticing how good he looked in a tank top. She peeped how he'd been drinking a lot lately but she knew it was the wrong time to talk about his up and coming flaws.

"You needed a tan, I see," Wolf said as she laid in her chair looking sexy in her little bikini.

"Facts. But did your people get the product I sent?"

"Yes, babe, but how you feeling - and be honest?" Wolf asked.

"I don't want to talk about that, to be honest. Let's just enjoy Miami and spend the night making love papi."

"Okay, mami," Wolf said, rubbing her feet making her smile.

"I'm straight, boo."

Chapter 26
Miami, FL

Rachela and two homegirls she had known for a while who lived in Miami were out to get a tan. For the past few months she had been traveling through New York to Miami on a regular basis. She loved Miami. The only problem was her rival Julie ran the city so whenever she came out to Miami, Rachela would lay low. Rachela always had the goons somewhere lurking and watching her but today she wanted to come out alone because her two girlfriends didn't know about her dangerous life.

Walking on the beach, she saw people all over the beach like roaches enjoying the beautiful day. Looking to her far left, she thought her eyes were playing tricks on her.

"Paris, I left your car door unlocked," Rachela told her pretty friend, who was black and eye candy and about to become a lawyer.

"I have to lock it, girl, that's a new Benz. These South Miami dudes will steal the rims off my shit." Paris turned to rush back to her car to lock it.

"Sorry!" Rachela yelled.

"Cara, can you go buy us some drinks?" Rachela said, handing Cara two hundred dollars.

"Damn, girl." Cara took the money and ran off.

Now that her girls were gone, she focused her attention on Keiline and Wolf. Rachela placed a hat on her head, which she had in a Birkin bag she carried. She then pulled out a big-ass chrome Glock 45 pistol with a grip.

Boc! Boc! Boc! Boc! Boc! Boc!

Keiline and Wolf both looked at the direction the shots were being fired while everybody ducked and ran everywhere, yelling. Wolf grabbed Keiline as they both saw a bad Latin woman in a bikini aiming for them.

"Bitch!" Keiline yelled, seeing it was Rachela.

Keiline and Wolf made a safe exit out to the parking lot to see two black SUVs pull up and men hop out with assault rifles. Wolf thought the men were for them until they ran past them and went for Rachela, who was now in the middle of the crowd shooting.

Tat! Tat! Tat! Tat! Tat! Tat!

Bullets from a Draco separated the crowd as the goons tried to take Rachela out. Rachela knew her handgun had no chance of winning against Dracos so she did what she knew and ran. The goons saw Rachela was gone with the crowd so they got back in the SUVs and left the same way they came.

The shooters were Julie people she knew everybody who touched down in her city. Keiline and Wolf made it back to the hotel, talking about the recent event.

***

Manhattan, NY

J Balla just had to go see a lawyer for his old head, who had been locked up for twenty years. When J Balla was upstate in prison he used to spin the yard with the OG and tell him one day he would get him an appeal lawyer so he could get out. When most niggas got money they would forget about niggas in the struggle, but J Balla was for the struggle. He had to meet SK Balla in Brooklyn so he and a few goons were sliding out there right now.

Chapter 27
Harlem, NY

OG and Rocky both climbed out of luxury cars in front of a well-known park downtown near Lexington.

"Why the long face?" OG asked Rocky, fixing his suit and tie. OG's appearance was boss status now so he rocked suits and ties to look like a true business man.

"What the fuck is going on with dem cats you told me about?" Rocky said with a loud, frustrated tone in his voice.

"How about you calm that tough guy shit down before I calm it down for you," OG said seriously.

"Maybe."

"Now who are you referring to, the kid Wolf?"

"Yes," Rocky said.

"I gotta switch gears into Plan B," OG stated.

"A'ight."

"Unless you have a solid plan to take him out, because the kid is a different type of animal," OG tried to warn him.

"I am an animal too, son," Rocky shot back.

"I know, Rocky, that's why you on the team, killer," OG gassed him up.

"I'm going to do my research. I know some people from Yonkers. That's where you say he from, right?" Rocky asked his plug.

"Yes sir."

"I'm on it."

"Okay, do that and get back at me," OG said.

"I got you, son." Rocky made a call as he walked off.

OG got in his car, thinking of a plan to get Wolf out of the picture so he could take over Yonkers and Westchester County.

***
San Juan, P.R.

MeMe was chilling in a beach resort in a silk robe with Dior slippers, looking into the crystal clean water on the beach outside of the resort. She needed this small vacation to get her mind right because she had a lot going on upstairs in her head and she was emotional. Losing her grandma was like a punch to the heart, but she wasn't going to let that hold her up in any way. Having Knight around at her times of need made her look at him differently now. She hadn't shared her bed with a man in years. Knight was that special man she had been waiting for. She knew why they called him Knight now.

"You okay, baby?" Knight walked on the balcony shirtless in a pair of Fendi shorts and Fendi slippers to match his drip.

"Yep."

"What happened to breakfast in bed?" he asked.

"You know how to dial room service," she joked.

"Damn, I ain't going no more." Knight hugged her curvy frame, loving every inch of her body.

"You always gang-gang, baby." She kissed his lips as they saw dolphins swimming in the ocean doing tricks.

"You been hanging around me too much," he said, laughing.

***

Harlem, NY

Behadi had come out to get her hair done at an African hair shop. She parked the Benz G Wagon SUV and got out in boy shorts, showing a little skin. A few dudes walked by and couldn't help but stare at her sexy feathers. She paid them no mind as she walked inside the hair salon, knowing she was the shit. Her appointment wasn't for ten more minutes and her stylist had someone in the chair already, so she sat down texting Lil K.

Things were going well beside the little distractions, which were the Cubans. She knew sooner or later they would resurface, then boom! Her time to shine would pop up.

Chapter 28
Harlem, NY

After Rachela's shootout in Miami, she decided to come back to NYC and finish her task up here. Seeing Wolf made her blood boil, but seeing Keiline sent her overboard. Rachela saw the Miami shooting on the news because two people popped up dead. If it wasn't for the gunmen hopping out on her in Miami she knew she would have had Keiline and Wolf. She figured out the gunmen had to be Julie's people because nobody had that type of pull in the city except her and another woman.

Today was a chill day for her, so Rachela just wanted to get her hair and nails done. Her normal spot where she got her nails and hair done was closed, so she came to a well-known African salon. The salon parlor was huge inside and she saw a bunch of beautiful African American women, which made her a little jealous.

Growing up in Cuba, she was mostly used to seeing Latina women but now coming to the States, she was seeing so many different beautiful races - blacks, whites, Columbians, Chinese, Koreans, Africans, Haitians, and others daily. She sat down waiting for a seat to open up. She picked up a magazine and started to read.

***

Behadi was under the blow dryer for over twenty minutes and Lil K was calling, but she couldn't answer. One thing Behadi hated was when people called her when she was under the dryer getting her hair done. Minutes later, her hairstylist lifted the dryer and showed her the beautiful masterpiece.

"Oh wow," Behadi said, seeing her long curly pressed hair, giving her that sexy boost of confidence even though she knew she was already a big snack. Behadi just so happened to look in the larger mirror to lock eyes with Rachela.

"Fucking bitch!" Behadi yelled, pulling a handgun out of her Gucci purse.

Rachela had a weapon in her coat pocket, a small .380 special.

Boc! Boc! Boc! Boc! Boc! Boc!

Behadi shot Rachela in the left shoulder, making her drop her weapon in pain.

"Ahhhhhhhhh!" Rachela's gun flew across the floor.

All the women in the salon yelled while running for the door. Some crawled out of the hair salon, praying to make it out alive.

Boc! Boc! Boc!

Rachela had no luck finding her gun,

"Shit!" Rachela ducked a few more bullets from Behadi, who was shooting like a pro, hitting a worker.

Rachela ran out of the salon into the lot, hearing police sirens up the block. She was bleeding badly but it wasn't bad enough that she had to go to the hospital.

***

Brooklyn, NY

Knight was driving to his NJ home, thinking about everything that had been taking place in his life these past years. Finding out Jose killed his real dad was a surprise, but having Smoke pretend to be his dad hurt the most. Losing so many good men to the streets was a lifetime pain only street nigga feel. He missed his daughter Kamala and Valentine. He thought daily about all the pain he placed on her throughout the years.

Now he was starting to catch feelings for MeMe and he knew he had to focus on business and this war going on because niggas were coming for his crown. Knight wasn't gonna let up He had a plan to hold his crown down from niggas like D Fatal Brim.

Chapter 29
Bronx, NY

D Fatal Brim was uptown near White Plains Roads to meet a nigga who was moving weight in Mount Vernon, which was connected to the Bronx and Yonkers. Since being in New York, he had been feeling like he wasn't really getting the job done which he came to do. Marie was in their condo really driving him crazy all day and he had to get away from her. The other night he almost choked her over a bottle of wine he spilled on the couch. She went crazy on him. He never knew Mexican women were so crazy, but he realized any woman who was attached to someone could act crazy at times, especially on her period.

As he drove the Maserati SUV over pot holes, he hoped he didn't fuck up the factory wheels. His homies in NJ and Long Island were moving product for him, but his goal was to take over the Bronx. D Fatal Brim felt like he deserved the Bronx because he put his blood, sweat, and tears into the city. He even took a life sentence for the Bronx, so now he felt like he was entitled to it.

Going against Knight was the only thing that felt different. He kinda felt like a snake because at the end of the day, Knight was the only nigga ever there for him. He remembered back in the day he and Knight used to run in niggas' projects, stripping them ass naked to rob them.

While locked up, he felt like it was Knight's fault. Less got killed and he always kept that in the back of his head.

Driving into Mount Vernon, he made his way to the projects or a block called 7th and 3rd.

***

Mount Vernon, NY

"I'm telling you, cuz, this nigga big time," Kali said, standing in the back parking lot.

"What's his name again?" TT asked, standing next to his cousin, who had been blowing up his phone for days.

Kali told him he knew a nigga who needed fifty keys and wanted to open shop in Mount Vernon and Yonkers. TT and Chills both took over Mount Vernon with the help of their crew, Da Goonies.

"Brim," Kali said, seeing a black luxury SUV pull up with bright HD lights.

"That's him?"

"Yeah, come on." Kali was happy because the man who called himself Brim told him he would give Kali a hundred grand in cash just to set him up with the nigga who ran Mount Vernon.

The main reason why TT didn't fuck with Kali was because he was shiesty and got his own brother killed years ago. TT saw the man get out of the SUV in all-re. He couldn't get a good look at the man's face because it was dark out.

"Dark Fatal Brim," Kali said, walking to the man.

When TT heard the man's name, he knew who he was and he pulled out his hammer.

Boom! Boom! Boom! Boom! Boom! Boom! Boom! Boom!

D Fatal Brim jumped back in his car, backing up, knowing he just got set up. He saw TT running down on his car.

Boom! Boom!

His window shattered and bullets hit his passenger seat headrest.

When TT saw the Maserati SUV race off, he turned to his cousin Kali, who had a dumbfounded look on his face.

Boom!

TT shot the man in his head, killing him. He had no type of mercy for killing Kali because this could have been the perfect set-up in his eyes. Wolf had told TT and Chills about a man named D Fatal Brim out to kill Knight, his partner, so if a nigga had problems with Wolf, they had it with Yonkers and Mount Vernon.

* * *

Harlem, NY

Maryanna woke up with a million and one things on her mind, but mainly it was Wolf and Knight. She needed them dead. She trained Wolf very well so she knew how dangerous he was and could be.

OG was out of town in D.R. Maryanna had to do something quick before Wolf got a hold of her or OG.

Chapter 30
South Beach, Miami

Knight and J Balla slid out to Miami for All Star Weekend and were having a blast, but Knight had another objective for coming out here. Since his nephew got killed, he only saw Julie a few times and when he found out the same people who killed his daughter and baby mother killed his nephew, he wanted blood. Knight would never forget the day he got the call from Jose Martinez letting him know his family was killed.

At first he thought Jose was playing with his mind because he moved his family to Texas away from the mix of things. When he received a picture text showing his daughter's and baby mother's heads cut off, he knew it was serious.

Tonight he was turned up in a club called The Mansion.

"Yo son, I needed this shit because I been going brazy in da town," J Balla said, popping an expensive bottle of liquor he couldn't even pronounce.

"I'm glad you came out, son, facts. Since you been with the family, you've been loyal to our gang. You showed me shit that most niggas can't show to their own mother," Knight said.

"That's a fact, boy."

"Trust me, this is only the beginning my brother," Knight confirmed.

"I already know, brodie. I know da vibes now let's go toss some stacks at the sack chasing thots," J Balla said picking up two big stacks of ones.

"That sounds like a plan to me," Knight said, following J Balla to the stage, dripping in jewelry.

***

Yonkers, NY

Wolf was on his way to buy Keiline a Rolls Royce Dawn coupe with the soft top. He'd been around Keiline long enough to know when something was wrong with Keiline and she had been miserable. When he asked her what was wrong, she ignored him and went to sleep the other night.

Today was her birthday so he wanted to do something special, so what was bigger than a $230,000 luxury car? Later on he needed to go check on TT across town on Riverdale, but right now he was on his way to Gun Hill Road in the Bronx.

Stopping at a red light, he leaned over to feel his cell phone had slipped into the side of his door panel. He just so happened to look in his rearview mirror to see a navy blue Toyota on his bumper. When he saw a woman in heels hop out with an assault rifle, he got a good look at her and saw it was his auntie.

"Bitch!" Wolf yelled, seeing her lift the weapon with ease.

Tat! Tat! Tat! Tat! Tat! Tat! Tat! Tat!

Bullets busted the windows and tore through the car, hitting him in the upper shoulder, but it was only a small graze. Wolf raced off, busting a sharp left as Maryanna's gunfire stopped.

Wolf's shoulder was burning in pain. He wanted to pull over, but he thought against it just in case she was close. He knew she had to be following him since he touched down in Yonkers. He knew there was no such thing as family when a nigga was in the streets.

***

Maryanna was highly upset she missed her shot at killing her nephew, who had been causing her a big headache.

Driving back to Harlem, she got a call from OG, but left him on red because she didn't want to talk. Missing her targets was something she could never get used to or accept. She prayed to catch him lacking again.

Chapter 31
New York City, NY

Lil K came out to an upscale bar alone to drink and get away from Behadi for a few hours because she had been driving him crazy. He was drunk, but still aware of his surroundings and what was going on.

"Let me get another shot," Lil K told the bartender.

"Make that two, please," a beautiful woman said, pulling up a stool next to him.

Lil K looked at her and her sex appeal caught his attention, but he tried his best not to stare at her.

"It's okay to look," she said, not looking at him.

"You talking to me?"

"No, the person next to you," she said, now facing him.

Lil K was so wasted he looked to his right to see nobody. The bar was half-empty besides a few people fresh off of work trying to get their drink on.

"You climbing the wrong tree, little mami," he said as the bartender served them their drinks.

"I guess climbing trees isn't the only thing I love to climb," she said sexually. "Take me to your truck and you'll find out."

Lil K looked at her like she just said something in a different language. He wanted to ask how she knew he had a truck, but instead, he took her hand and went outside. Lil K entered his Range Rover and laid the seats down and she removed her thongs. The woman went for his pants and pulled out his dick and started sucking from the tip down while making slurping noises.

"Ummm," he moaned, leaning his head back as she went to work.

Controlling his nut was getting hard as she deep throated his whole cock without gagging. She stopped and climbed on his pipe and his penis loosened up her tight walls.

"Ooohhh yesss," she moaned, slow grinding, letting his pipe adjust to her sex walls.

The pussy was so good that Lil K nutted inside of her as she rode his dick like she was riding a bull. It took a few seconds for her to climax. She kissed his lips passionately and whispered in his ear.

"You will always be on my mind no matter what happens," she said, climbing off his dick, leaving a water puddle on his floor.

Lil K wanted to stop the sexy chick from leaving, but his nut was so good his legs were numb. He saw her climb in a new luxury car, pulling off while speeding. Lil K was starting to sober up as he remembered he didn't even find out her name. Getting dressed, he felt something poke his feet and it was the woman's gold earring. The earring had a name on it.

"Aliza," he said out loud, reading the letters on the earring. He tried to think back to where he'd heard the name from.

Before he pulled out of the lot, it came to him. Aliza was Rachela's sister.

"Fuck." He couldn't believe he just made love to an opp. Lil K couldn't stop thinking about how good her pussy was and how he had just cheated on his wife.

***

Yonkers, NY

Chills had goons standing on each corner on Elm Street pitching crack to the local fiends trying to spend their first of the month checks on drugs.

"Yo Russ, pull up son," Chills called the youngest nigga on the block, hopping off his sport bike.

"Nice bike, Chills."

"Good looks. But what's on out here?" Chills asked.

Russ was only fourteen so Chills didn't let him sell drugs. Instead, he made him his personal eyes and ears. Chills made sure he only worked after school hours from 3 p.m. to 8 p.m.

"Dugg got shot up two nights ago on London Street at 6:40 p.m. and JRoc told the police everything when they ran down on him and the guys. He was the only one they didn't arrest," Russ said.

"Where is JRoc now?"

"Somewhere in Harlem. Now he working for some bad bitch," Russ said.

"What are you talking about?"

"Oh, yesterday some sexy chick pulled up in a Wraith offering niggas $10,000 to join her crew in Harlem. I guess they getting money." Russ shrugged his shoulders.

Chills knew it had to be that Spanish bitch Maryanna.

"A'ight, I gotta go, but hold this shit down," Chills said before pulling off.

Romell Tukes

Chapter 32
City Island, Bronx

Knight drove his new all-white Rolls Royce Cullinan down the long strip filled with seafood spots. Since he was a kid, Knight and his crew loved coming down here to eat and bag bitches. Driving down to the end, old memories started to dawn on him when Kip Loc, Black, Less, Paco, and Kazzy Loc were all alive and turning up the city.

The strong smell of fresh food filled the night air as he pulled into the car lot to see his little brother's black Bentley Continental GT V8. Lil K called him a few days ago informing him he ran into a big problem, but he knew better to talk crazy over the phone.

"Yeroooo!" Knight shouted with his NY accent.

"What up?" Lil K's voice was flat and dry as he leaned on his car eating fish.

"I hate coming down here, bro, because something always happens. I remember our first shoot out down here," Knight stated, looking into the water.

"Yeah, that's facts, but we got a minor problem," Lil K said.

"What else is new?"

"Look at this." Lil K handed him the earring Aliza left in his SUV days ago.

"What the fuck is this?" Knight said, looking at the name on the gold earring.

"Aliza, that bitch's sister. You don't remember?"

"Oh shit, Rachela's sister? How you get this?" Knight asked.

"Long story."

"Long story? Nigga, what happened?" Knight knew it was more than what he was hearing.

"I was drunk and she slid on me in the bar. One thing led to another and I fucked her raw and she said shit that fucked me up."

"What?"

"She said I will always be on her mind no matter what happens," Lil K told him as he thought back to how good her pussy was. He felt bad and guilty because he was married to a good woman.

"Why she ain't kill you? That's weird," Knight said, puzzled.

"I don't know, but there was something about her that stood out from Rachela, bro."

"Rachela fucked me then used me, bro. Them bitches is mind masters. I'm just glad she ain't smoke you."

"Facts."

"You slippin', son. What the fuck is really going on?" Knight's question didn't even have time to get answers before five gunmen started to let off shots.

Bloc! Bloc! Bloc! Bloc! Bloc! Bloc! Bloc!

Knight blocked Lil K and made it to his gun on time to see a nigga creeping up behind him. Knight fired two shots in the man's head as Lil K was now busting off shots at the shooters to see one familiar face.

"Knight, that's D Fatal Brim!" Lil K yelled as Knight spun around to see D Fatal Brim a few feet away from him with a Tech 9 submachine gun aimed at him.

Tat! Tat! Tat! Tat!

Knight ducked low, dodging his childhood friend's gunfire. Lil K hit two more of D Fatal Brim shooters, but what he saw next made him freeze. Knight and Lil K saw Marie pop the trunk to a Maserati sedan and pull out a baby rocket launcher. Both brothers looked at each other and ran for the water, jumping over a small railing into the water.

BOOMMMM!

The blast blew up eight cars and killed four people parked in their cars hiding from the gunfire. Mostly all the civilians were in the restaurant eating and enjoying their meal.

D Fatal Brim and Marie got away from the scene thinking Lil K and Knight were dead because they didn't see them jump into the water.

***

Ten minutes later, Knight and Lil K climbed out of the water onto a board walk. They were drenched in water. Lil K was breathing hard, outta wind from swimming, something he hated, but to his surprise, Knight was good at it.

"You good?" Knight asked, checking to see if he still had his phone, which was waterproof. He kept it tucked in the pocket of his thermals.

"Nah, nigga, a Mexican bitch just tried to kill me with a fucking bazooka!" Lil K shouted.

"I don't even know how we got caught out there like that, bro." Knight called J Balla to come pick them up from Co-op City.

"I'm gonna kill that nigga."

"I can't believe he getting down like that and that shawty who tried to take us out was his wife," Knight said.

"They both dead."

"Facts, word to Mommy's grave," Knight said, walking up the street near the highway.

Romell Tukes

Chapter 33
Manhattan, NY

Marie's body collapsed on the king-sized bed after getting fucked for close to an hour straight. D Fatal Brim had her climax six times, and her body couldn't take any more. Tonight, letting off that big-ass rocket did something to her that sparked a newfound energy in her.

"I did good, huh baby?" she asked as he laid there next to her outta energy.

"Yeah, but I didn't tell you to do that."

"I thought you needed my help, papi?" she whined.

"I would've asked you, Marie. That's your problem now. You don't listen to me at all." He was trying not to get upset.

"I'm sorry."

"Are you?"

"I am, daddy, and let me show you how sorry I am," she said, going down toward his manhood.

She started slapping his penis on her face before sucking the tip then going crazy, spitting and slurping as tears formed in her eyes while she gagged. They eventually went for round two.

***

South Bronx, NY

J Balla was spending time with his new girlfriend Ari, a sexy thick dark-skinned woman who was a big-time model and video vixen. Ari was born and raised in Harlem, but she now lived in the Upper Westside of the city. Tonight, they were spending time with each other. Since she was on her period, sex was out of the question, so talking and building was the next best thing.

"I have a question," Ari asked, sitting up in the bed, pausing the movie they were watching.

"What, babe?"

"I'm taking you serious and you know I don't want to play games or have to worry about you going to jail like my ex," she said.

J Balla already knew what Ari was getting at. He knew her boyfriend before he went off to prison for drug selling, which got him a life sentence, and she almost got in some serious shit. Ari also worked for the IRS, so she had a good job and didn't want to risk her career again for dealing with a hustler.

"I feel you."

"That's all?"

"What you want me to say, babe?" J Balla shot back, already knowing where this was going again.

"My brother is still in Harlem hustling, and I don't even talk to Rocky, so if you don't get your shit together, I'm out," Ari told him.

J Balla was stuck on the name Rocky. He remembered a dude from Harlem named Rocky doing big things.

"You never told me you had a brother," J Balla said.

Ari just looked at him before going to the bathroom talking to herself, pissed off at him.

***

Uptown, Bronx

Behadi used Lil K's Range because he was using her car and she wanted to go grocery shopping today before he came back from New Jersey. Since Knight went on a small vacation, Lil K was left to handle everything. She hated that, but she knew it was his job. She just wished he would focus back on his deen as Muslim because he was lacking.

Pulling into the shopping center, she grabbed her gun from under the driver seat to feel something else: clothing fabric. She pulled out a thong and stared at it, knowing it wasn't hers. She knew Lil K never let anybody drive his truck except her so he had to have someone else in the car with him.

The pain she felt was hurt and betrayal. She didn't even want to shop. She drove home and spent the rest of her evening crying and stressing.

Romell Tukes

Chapter 34
Santos, Brazil

Knight needed a vacation and so did MeMe. She was overloaded with her work. She had clients all over the world and Knight was one of the few.

They parked the jet skis on the sand connected to a spectacular resort in a deep-water wide canal basin.

"That was fun." MeMe hopped off the jet ski, walking onto the private beach area. She looked sexy in her Chanel two-piece bikini with her nice ass out and perfect breasts.

"Facts," Knight stated, sitting down, taking off his watch. He didn't realize he got soaked.

"You and this facts word," MeMe said in her strong Spanish accent.

"Do you miss me?" he asked her, rubbing her thighs, loving her smooth skin.

"Should I?"

"Yes."

"Oh yeah? Why should I? You're not my man," she said, smiling, pushing his hand away. MeMe was starting to feel like their relationship was based on sex, even though they only had sex twice.

"I've been doing a lot of thinking, mami."

"I can't wait to hear this, papi." She sat up, paying close attention to him, something he really liked about her.

At times, she reminded him of his late baby mother, Valentine.

"I really like you, MeMe, since I first laid eyes on you. I'm used to dealing with my sexy black women so dealing with a Latina woman is new to me, and I like everything about you," he said.

"That's all?"

"No. I love your personality and I want to really make this work if you give me a chance. I don't want to mix our affairs with our business foundation, you know," he said.

"Oh, believe me, papi, you will never come between my business, so you don't even have to worry about that." She got serious.

"I want to take this to another level."

"Can I trust you?" She really judged people off their actions and he never showed her any type of shady or grimy shit, so she had respect for him.

"Hell yeah, and I'll do whatever to prove to you I'm loyal," Knight said, looking into her colorful eyes.

"If I were to tell you someone in your circle is crossing you, what would you do?"

"I'll kill them. Where is this going, ma?" Now Knight's mind was wandering at fast speed.

"Just a question, Knight," she shot back.

"You sure?"

"Yeah. But I'm happy to be your baby now and if I catch you cheating, I'm gonna cut your balls off," she joked.

"You dead-ass serious?"

"Yep." She kissed his lips as they rolled around on the beach.

They had a whole weekend with each other and now since they made things official, they both had a different outlook on each other.

***

Gun Hill, Bronx

SK Balla and two of his goons were in a pool hall drinking and chilling, about to leave. SK had been seeing a big bag dealing with J Balla. He was now able to feed his goons from Cortland all the way to Castle Hill projects.

"We about to bounce, son," SK told A.I.

"A'ight, I'm waiting on North. She get off in an hour," A.I. said, referring to his girlfriend who was a bartender.

"Say less, Blood," SK Balla said as he took his cup of Patron, walking out of the club with Bigger Balla, his right-hand man.

SK Balla had to meet up with J Balla in Queens tomorrow for a meeting so he was planning to go home and go to sleep.

Walking across the street, they were blinded by headlights and a car ran into them both going 25mph, knocking both down. SK

Balla groaned in pain as he moved to see four men jump out of the car and D Fatal Brim was leading the pack.

"Damn, Blood, that was a hard hit. I'm gonna make sure I send your mama some teddy bears," D Fatal Brim said.

Boom! Boom! Boom! Boom!

D Fatal Brim killed him and got back in the car, pulling off with his goons.

Romell Tukes

Jack Boys vs Dope Boys

Chapter 35
New York City, NY

Lil K took Behadi out to eat at a classy restaurant where everybody was dressed in business attire and expensive outfits. Behadi looked stunning in her Louis Vuitton dress and red bottom heels, showing off her pretty toes. Lil K could tell something was wrong with her because she'd been acting funny all week. He thought by taking her out to eat she would feel a little better to get out of the house but now he saw that wasn't the case at all.

"What's up with you?" he finally asked, breaking the ice.

"What you mean what's up with me?" she shot back, giving him the evil eye.

"You know what I mean." He saw she stopped eating.

"You want me to be real?"

"Yes please."

"Okay, who recently used your truck?" She crossed her arms.

"My Range Rover?"

"Nah, dummy, your G5 airplane. You know what truck," she spat back loudly as people around them looked their way, being nosy.

"Nobody used my truck, baby, facts," he said with honesty.

"Oh, so that means these belong to you? Either you're a vicious cross dresser or a cheater." She pulled out the thong she found in the SUV and tossed it at him.

When Lil K saw the thong, he thought she was bugging. "Where you get this from?"

"Your fucking truck!"

"What? I don't——" Lil K paused, remembering Aliza that night.

"It finally hit you, huh. Find your way home. Better yet, go find that bitch. And she had a brown stain in her thong, you nasty bitch!" Behadi yelled, picking up a glass of water and threw it on him before she got up to leave.

Lil K couldn't believe what just took place. He didn't even have a chance to defend himself. He knew Behadi needed a few days to calm down and think shit through.

***

Rachela pulled up to the classy restaurant to grab a decent meal. She hoped they had Spanish food inside. She parked and saw a new Bentley race past, her almost hitting her rear end.

"Bitch!" Rachela yelled to the car as she walked towards the restaurant she had Googled.

Wolf and Keiline were outta town again so she was left alone in NY, but she'd been going to the gym and exercising to burn some time. Walking in the lobby, the first person she saw was Lil K coming her way like he was leaving. When he locked eyes with the woman, he knew who she was and they both pulled out weapons and started to fire.

Boc! Boc! Boc! Boc! Bloc! Bloc! Bloc!

Customers were yelling, screaming, and crawling for the back exit. Some jumped out of the windows trying to get away from the city shit.

Boc! Boc!

Lil K jumped over a table, feeling a burn to his leg, but he was worried about Rachela getting up close on him with his big gun. He couldn't front, she was looking sexy letting off that big-ass chrome 50 Cal handgun. Lil K popped up firing but his gun jammed and when Rachela saw this, a smile appeared on her face before she fired two more rounds, making him duck.

Boc! Boc!

"Don't run, handsome!" she yelled, seeing him go for the window, but she followed in her heels letting off shots.

Lil K flew out the window and dipped out of the parking lot as cars drove wildly all over the place, almost smashing into each other.

Behadi was parked across the street watching the whole scene. When she saw Lil K running across the street, she blew her horn at him and flashed her lights. He saw it was her and got inside to see her smiling. He didn't say a word as she pulled off.

"You saw the whole shit?" he asked when she got on the highway.

"You talking to me?"

"Yeah."

"I saw Rachela in the parking lot when I was leaving," she said.

"Why you ain't tell me?"

"I forgot."

"You was sitting right here." He was getting tight.

"So what?"

"You got it."

"Next time, don't cheat," she told him.

"You don't even know what happened. It was that bitch's sister. I was drunk at a bar and she manhandled me and raped me."

"You expect me to believe that?"

"I really don't care if you do or don't. I never lied to you," Lil K stated, knowing he had to put an extra spin on what really happened.

Behadi was quiet, in deep thought.

Chapter 36
Miami, FL

Julie waited in a Colombian restaurant for MeMe to arrive so they could have another sit down to discuss the big problem they were both having with Rachela. Every time Julie thought about that bitch Rachela she would think about her late son who was murdered. Knowing the person who killed her son was still out there made her feel like less of a woman. She liked MeMe a lot and they both were trying to join forces since MeMe popped up at her home a while back after Julie lost her son.

MeMe walked in the spot, leaving her security outside. She looked comfortable in her white designer jumpsuit with high heels.

"Nice tan," MeMe said, sitting down, taking off her frames.

"Thanks. You look nice," Julie repeated.

"I was already out here with my man so meeting up with you was already part of my plans," MeMe said.

"You're in a relationship?" Julie loved being nosy.

"Yes and I'm in a very happy space." MeMe smiled thinking about Knight.

"You should have brought him along. We like family."

"Next time. How's our situation coming out?" MeMe asked.

"The last time I heard she was out here I sent my man to take care of Rachela, but the hoe got away." Julie shook her head.

"I believe she's been in New York a lot."

"Knight's turf."

"Yeah. I think she's after his operations or him," MeMe started looking at a text on her phone from Knight.

"Whatever it is, I may have to send some men up there," Julie said.

"Let me know because I have my people on it as we speak."

"In New York?" Julie asked, a little shocked.

"Yeah."

"Oh that's good. Normally Knight doesn't let anybody enter his city with ease," Julie replied.

"When times change, people do. I will keep you updated. Whenever you send your people. Let me know so our goons can link up," MeMe said before getting up to leave.

"Sure."

***

South Miami, FL

Knight came out to do some shopping at one of the big malls in the city while his girl MeMe was out. His relationship with MeMe was going well. She turned out to be a sweetheart, but tough on the outside. MeMe had everything he always wanted in a woman. The only issue was he felt less of a man copping drugs from his girlfriend and she had just raised the price on him.

He walked out of the Chanel store. He was ready to leave and head back to his condo where he stayed whenever he came to Miami. He told MeMe the history of him and Julie but also the history of his late brother Kazzy Loc and Julie. He told MeMe about his nephew that was killed so MeMe understood what was going on. Even though he had never fucked Julie, he wanted to keep it real with MeMe because he felt like she deserved that, at least.

He left the mall through the main entrance, hating the scorching heat that burned his skin. Two GMC SUV's pulled up and gunmen jumped out with big ass guns.

Tat! Tat! Tat!

Knight tossed his bags and hit the ground, getting out his weapon. When he popped up to shoot back, he saw three vans pull up.

"Fuck," he said, thinking he was about to die.

To his surprise, the men with dreads and Haitian flags jumped out firing at the men who came for Knight.

Bloc! Bloc!

Knight shot one of the men who climbed out of the truck. He ran down on him.

130

"Who sent you, bitch?" Knight said as the last two men standing hopped back in the truck, racing off away from the Haitians.

"Rachela!" the man cried before Knight put two in his head.

"Stephan sends her regards to you," one of the Haitians said before hopping back in the van and racing off.

Romell Tukes

Chapter 37
Yonkers, NY

TT left his sister's crib, laughing at how crazy she was. His sister was a recovering addict, so he'd been taking care of her since she got outta rehab. Things in Yonkers had been good. His team was eating and that's all he cared about.

Crossing the dark street, he saw a person get out of a van, which caused him to focus his attention on the van. Wolf told TT and Chills to watch their backs because there was a lot of shit going on and he needed them to be on point. He was so busy looking at the man in front of him he didn't see the person creeping up behind him.

Whack!

A long metal object knocked TT out, leaving his head busted on the cement.

***
Uptown, Harlem

A half hour later TT opened his eyes to see darkness but that was the pillowcase. He was tied up on the floor, unable to move. He smelled piss and he heard dogs barking out loudly.

"Yonkers in the building," a voice said, snatching off TT's head cover.

OG and Maryanna stood in front of him.

"What the fuck y'all want?" TT stated, showing no signs of fear.

"We just want to talk," Maryanna said with a sweet voice as if she wasn't the one who had knocked him out.

TT looked around to realize he was in a pit where dogs fought. "Talk about what, bitch?"

"Wolf," Maryanna shot back.

"Who the fuck is Wolf?" TT said before Maryanna kicked him in his nuts.

"Ahhh," TT gritted in pain, feeling the pain in his stomach.

"Who does Wolf work for?" OG asked, running low on patience.

"El Chapo," TT said with a smirk, hearing his phone go off.

"This one thinks it's a game," Maryanna said, picking up his phone to see it was a missed call from Chills.

"Kill him and toss his body in the Hudson River," OG said, walking off.

Boc! Boc! Boc! Boc! Boc!

She killed TT and answered his ringing phone.

***

Mount Vernon, NY

Chills had been calling TT for an hour to see if he wanted to go out to a club in Queens. TT finally picked up his phone.

"Damn, son, what, you in some good pussy?" Chills asked.

"TT is no longer with us, Chills, but why don't you save yourself?" Maryanna said.

"What? Who the fuck is this playing on my bro's phone?" Chills thought it was one of TT's bitches playing on his phone because it happened twice before.

"This is no child's play, Chills. You're next," Maryanna said before the phone went dead.

Chills couldn't believe his boy was dead now after all the work they put in together.

"What's good, Chills?" one of his boys asked, coming into the crib.

"They killed TT."

"Our TT?"

"Yeah," Chills said, getting up to leave, feeling fucked up over the news.

***

Manhattan, NY

Marie was in the condo pacing back and forth, wondering how she was going to tell her husband she was pregnant. She found out earlier she was five to six weeks pregnant, and she was against abortion. Marie wanted to see where D Fatal Brim's head was at because she knew he had a lot going on with trying to take over the New York streets. At times she wished he would just be okay with running the drug trade in L.A., but he seemed too greedy, and she knew that could be his downfall. His downfall would also be her downfall because she was his ride or die.

D Fatal Brim walked into the crib, exhausted from his long night out on the town.

"Hey babe." She jumped in his arms. She remembered he used to be so big while he was in prison.

"What you doing up?"

"I ain't know I had a bedtime, babe," she stated, following him into the kitchen.

"Okay, smart mouth. What's up? How was your day?"

"I have good news," she said with an excited spirit.

"What's that?" He took a sip of water out of a bottle he had left out a few days ago.

"I'm pregnant, babe," she said with a bright smile.

"Right now?"

"Yes."

"Oh, that's good. I'm going to sleep." He walked off, leaving her very upset and confused.

Years ago while in jail, he used to always talk about kids, but now it was a different story.

Romell Tukes

Chapter 38
White Plains, NY

Wolf had recently moved Keiline to a classy building in an upscale area in Westchester County. Keiline was leaving her apartment to go out to grab a bite to eat from a Cheesecake Factory that had good food. Wolf was in Harlem running around somewhere on his paper chase. Every night he would come home close to midnight and she wouldn't say a word.

Tomorrow she was heading back to Costa Rica for a few days. She had her child with her now asleep in her arms, waiting for the elevator. Having her daughter with her was a handful.

She took the elevator to the basement lower garage area where all the residents' cars were parked. She disliked living in New York, but she liked the big city for a vacation vibe. Putting her daughter in the back seat of the Benz G Wagon truck, she heard something. She closed the door and pulled out her weapon, looking for any surprise visitors. Keiline didn't see the man creeping behind.

Boc! Boc! Boc! Boc!

The man was a few feet to her rear as she clocked him and let off two rounds back. The shooter was so swift the way he moved that Keiline knew the man was the same type of professional killer. Keiline saw a dark-skinned pretty woman with an AR 15 sneaking up behind the man trying to kill her.

Tat! Tat! Tat! Tat!

Keiline saw Behadi standing over the Hispanic man with her gun to his head.

"Silent, I remember you," Behadi said as Keiline walked up.

"Who sent you to kill me?" Keiline asked the killer, who was now in a puddle of blood.

"Jose, and you and your sister will die," Silent said as his vision started to fade away.

Behadi shot him twice in the head.

"You good?" Behadi asked Keiline, who looked in her truck to see that her daughter was still sound asleep.

"Yes. Thank you so much for saving me."

"No problem, but I had no clue he was coming for you," Behadi said as the AR-15 hung from her hand, almost dragging on the ground.

"You know him?" Keiline asked.

"Yes. He's a vicious hitman for Jose and other Cuban families. I heard he was in town, so I figured he was coming for my man or Knight," Behadi heard sirens.

"Thanks again. I have to go. I'm going to be in touch." Keiline heard the sirens also so she wanted to get away.

"A'ight." Behadi ran through the garage, hopping on Lil K's bike and pulling off.

**

Atlantic City, NJ

J Balla waited at a hotel room for his guest. He had the place set up nicely. He was nervous about tonight because the woman who was coming to see him had his heart. J Balla's girlfriend's Ari and him were going through it right now, so his side chick was his next best thing. The knock on the door had him jump up, looking around to make sure everything was set up neatly.

"Hey you." Rachela walked into the room rocking a long pea coat with heels.

J Balla and Rachela had been on the low for over a year now since he met her in D.R. on vacation. The two had been vibing since and building in every way.

"Damn, baby," he said as she opened up her coat to see her fat, shaved pussy and perfect body.

"You been sticking to the plan?" Rachela said in a sexy voice as J Balla went low on her.

"Of course, baby," J Balla said before burying his face in her dripping pussy.

Chapter 39
Cuba

Jose Martinez waited on his daughter to arrive so he could get in her ass about what had been going on in New York. He was very disappointed in the way shit was turning out. He thought taking care of Knight and the Costa Rican sisters would be a piece of cake.

Jose saw Rachela come in the crib on his monitor from the living room TV. As soon as Rachela walked in, he put his blunt out and stood up. Rachela thought her dad was about to give her a hug as always.

"Hey papi," she said, only to see his hand cock block as he slapped the shit outta her. Rachela's body flew into the wall. "Daddy!" she yelled, holding her busted mouth.

"You don't fucking listen. I told you to go to New York and take care of that situation, not make a big mess," he said, going to sit down on the Fendi couch.

"I'm trying, Father," she said, fixing her hair.

"Try harder, bitch!" he shouted.

"I almost got him, Daddy," she stated.

"Where is your sister?"

"I don't know," Rachela said, telling the truth because she hadn't seen Aliza in months.

"Get out of my house and don't come back until you have taken care of our problem," Jose told her, dismissing her.

Rachela left the house upset, but she knew what needed to be done. She started to wonder where Aliza was now that Jose brought it to her head. J Balla had been updated on Knight and Lil K's events but she knew if them niggas found out, it would be all bad.

***

Harlem, NY

Chills made his way to Harlem to pay his brother a visit. He hated him, but he needed to hear him out because he was still blood.

His grandma called him last night begging him to make amends with his brother because life was short.

Driving through Harlem, he was on his way to 116th Street to make his brother next to a big time mosque. Minutes later, he pulled up to the mosque to see brothers walking in and out. Out of all places to meet, he wondered why here, but then he saw a big body Jaguar pull up with tints. He assumed it was his brother, so he got out and leaned on the front of his Hellcat.

***

Rocky got out dripping in ice, looking like a crystal ball. His grandma brought the two brothers together today. If it wasn't for her, he wouldn't even have given Chills a second of his time.

"What up, son?" Chills said.

"What's going on?" Rocky asked, looking at Chills.

"I ain't even wanna pull up on you, but I did it for Grandma," Chills said.

"Same here, my nigga, but regardless, we blood so I'm willing to let bygones be bygones, bro," Rocky said.

"So we good?"

"That's a fact," Rocky shot back.

"We locked in, I guess." Chills gave his brother dap.

"I heard you getting money?" Rocky asked.

"Yeah, I been on the grind in Yonkers," Chills said.

Rocky grew up in Harlem while Chills grew up in the heart of Yonkers.

"You know a nigga named Wolf?" Rocky asked.

"Yeah, that's my plug," Chills said, realizing from the look on his brother's face he said too much.

"Chills, I'm going to kill this nigga when I see him!" Rocky shouted.

"What happened?"

"Dat nigga been robbing my spots and trying to kill me," Rocky said.

"You sure it was Wolf?" Chills played dumb.

"Nigga, hell yeah! I need you to help me get son."

Chills paused because Wolf was more of a brother than Rocky was to him, but Rocky was blood.

"Give me some time to figure this shit out."

"What is there to figure out, son?" Rocky asked.

"Give me some time." Chills walked off, getting in his car.

Romell Tukes

Chapter 40
North Miami, FL

Julie got a call from a powerful cartel family in Mexico asking her to meet up with a highly-respected cartel leader. Being respectful, she accepted the meeting and now she was waiting for her guest in the hotel restaurant near Collins Avenue. Julie had been hearing rumors that Stephen, her number two enemy, was back in town. She wanted to be the only queenpin in town. There wasn't enough space in the city for two boss bitches. Julie didn't even know who was coming to visit her so she had a few goons lurking throughout the restaurant for her safety. Since losing her son, she had been extra overprotective of her own life and family.

Looking towards the door, she saw a nice-looking Mexican woman walking in the restaurant and towards her table.

"What the fuck is this?" Julie said, looking at the woman as she approached the table.

"Hey, I'm Marie from L.A. and the Gulf Cartel. I had my people reach out to you because I believe I can help you," Marie said.

"You and a million others," Julie said.

"Excuse me?"

"Look, Ms. Marie, I'm going to keep it real. I don't know you, but I do know we were connected while I was in Cali," Julie said.

"The Five Families? You're Julie? Oh my God!" Marie remembered who the woman was. They both had ties to one of the biggest organizations a few years back in Cali.

"I run my own shit, so please don't see me for that," she said to Marie.

"Okay, but my reason for coming down here is that I'm having a big problem trying to lock down the state of New York and I heard we have the same problem up there," Marie stated.

"Problem?" Julie wanted to make sure she heard correctly.

"Yes, enemy, a man named Knight who is dealing with the Costa Rican sisters," Marie said.

"Knight?"

"Yes, he is getting product from the sisters," Marie said, seeing a surprised look on Julie's face.

"I have no clue as to what you're talking about, but I believe you heard wrong," Julie said.

"So you not trying to help me?" Marie asked.

"How about I do this…" Julie paused, seeing Marie smile.

"I knew you would see my vision," Marie said.

"I'm going to give you twenty-three hours to get out of my city and never bring your bean-eating ass back down here," Julie said.

"You're Mexican too," Marie said, upset, getting up to leave and feeling disrespected. If she could kill Julie right now in front of the few in the restaurant, she would.

Marie had no clue everybody in the restaurant were part of her goons. Marie got out of the spot quickly, not looking back.

Julie thought about what Marie just told her and was wondering if she could call Knight, since she had his old number.

***

Fishkill, NY

Knight's mansion upstate was quiet and peaceful. He loved coming up here when he needed to get away from the city. MeMe was in the master bedroom asleep. He was up at 5 a.m. exercising, doing burpees with push ups and light weights.

Last night he got a call from Julie informing him of a woman named Marie trying to line him up, but she made it clear she was on his side. When she asked about him and MeMe, he told her they were deeply involved and there was a long pause on the phone. Knight had a lot on his plate at the moment so he knew he couldn't do much to please her emotions. The relationship with him and MeMe was going smoothly and he didn't feel the need to hide it.

After his hard workout, he went to shower up and cook breakfast for MeMe.

***

Uptown, Bronx

Wolf came out to the Bronx to meet up with Lil K to see how things were going businesswise. He pulled up to the White Castle fast food spot to grab a bite to eat, thinking about how weird Chills was acting. He climbed out of his car to see Chill's car entering the lot. He wondered what he was doing in the Bronx. He waved Chills down, happy to see his boy. He wanted to talk to him anyway about why he was acting funny. The Hellcat passenger window rolled down and Wolf leaned over to see Chills raising a gun. Wolf took off running.

Boc! Boc! Boc! Boc!

Chills jumped out of his car to fire two more rounds, but missed Wolf, who was almost across the street. He was pissed that he missed the target and now he had to be on extra point because Wolf saw him. Chills was riding with his brother Rocky against Wolf because Chills knew blood was forever.

Romell Tukes

Chapter 41
New York City, NY

Aliza had turned into a party animal. All she did was party and have sex every night with strange men. The lounge she was at tonight was filled with people coming out to have a good time for the holiday weekend. She knew her dad and sister would be mad at her if they found out what was going on with her. A big secret she didn't have the chance to share with people was that she was pregnant. She'd only had unprotected sex with one person in the past few months and that was Lil K that night after the club.

For the past hour she'd been posted up at the bar drinking shots of Patron. Even though she was pregnant she didn't let it stop her from drinking

"Two more shots," she asked the bartender.

"You sure, Miss? You already fucked up," the bartender dude said over the loud noise in the club.

"Two more," she said, about to vomit all over the bar.

Aliza got up and went to the restroom rushing into the empty stall. She started throwing up in the toilet and on the floor.

"Oh my fucking God," she said, taking a breather.

When she stood up, Behadi stood behind her with a gun pointed at her face.

"Judgment day," Behadi said.

"Who the fuck are you?" Aliza said, wiping the vomit off her mouth.

"I'm da bad-ass bitch who's about to kill your whore ass." Behadi saw all the green vomit on the floor.

"Where?"

"You fucked my man, bitch."

"Lil K?" Aliza laughed, trying to stand straight because she was so drunk.

"It's funny, huh, bitch?"

"He liked it, and I'm pregnant too, you dumb bitch," Aliza said, seeing Behadi's face light up with anger.

Boc! Boc! Boc! Boc! Boc!

Behadi sent the bullets right through her skull, killing her. Aliza's body collapsed on her own vomit. Behadi walked out of the club happy that the bathroom walls were soundproof.

***

Fishkill, NY

Knight and MeMe were both fixing the garden in the backyard, getting peace of mind.

"You're good at gardening, babe," MeMe stated.

"You being funny," Knight said.

"Nah, papi, I'm serious," she said, laughing, throwing dirt on him.

"You playing dirty, huh?" Knight tossed dirt back on her.

"I'm horny," she said, laying on her back with her booty shorts on and tank top.

"Me too." Knight crawled between her legs and wasted no time pulling out his hard on and slowly entering her tightness.

Knight and MeMe made love right there on the dirt in the small garden.

***

South Bronx

J Balla had a lot on his mind lately. Rachela wanted him to speed up his process of trying to find out Lil K's location. Rachela's pussy was so good he started having dreams about her while with his girlfriend.

He was driving to Castle Hill to see his workers. He hadn't seen Lil K in a few days and his mind started wandering. Having a guilty conscience was heavy on his mind lately and crossing Lil K was hurting him because he'd been nothing but good to him. J Balla knew if his brother M Balla was here, he would be disappointed in his disloyalty towards good men like Lil K and Knight.

Driving into the lot, he saw police all over the place. He saw one of his young boys out there.

"PH, what happened?" J Balla asked a young nigga.

"Somebody came through and killed seven people. It was a bitch," PH stated.

"What! When?"

"An hour ago," PH said.

"A'ight, close the shop and I'll see you tomorrow." J Balla got the fuck up outta there, wondering what happened.

Romell Tukes

Chapter 42
Harlem, NY

Rocky had a nice brownstone apartment near Lexington Avenue shopping area, which was known for its historical establishments. Earlier he was in an after hour club partying with his little brother and some of his goons. He was more than happy his little brother Chills picked his side to ride against Wolf.

Chills now lived in Harlem, but he was still making his rounds in Yonkers. Rocky was locking down the whole city of Harlem thanks to his plug. Life was good and he had no complaints at all and shit was sweet.

The loud doorbell woke him up from his sleep. He wasn't expecting any company, but he went to answer the door in his Gucci slippers and robe.

"Who the fuck bugging like this?" Rocky shouted, opening the door slowly to see Maryanna standing there in a sexy dress.

"Hey handsome, can I come in?" she said.

"Sure." He moved over, letting her inside, looking at her fat ass in her dress.

"I just stopped by to tell you how proud I am of you, Rocky," she said.

"I should be thanking you," he said as she closed in on him.

"You been on my mind lately," she said sexually.

"Who, me?" Rocky felt her hand grab his manhood.

"I been missing out." She laughed, sliding a gun out from her thigh holster.

"Let's go to the bedroom so I can show you," he said, kissing her neck.

"I got a better plan," she said, now pointing her gun at his forehead.

"You dirty bitch," he said.

"Feisty, daddy."

"Why me? I was loyal to you and OG." Rocky couldn't believe he let a bitch double cross him.

"Loyalty. I'm going to put you on game before I kill you. Loyalty will get you killed because you never know who you're being loyal to. How do you know what's in the next person's heart?" She spit knowledge.

"I can only go off what's in my heart. I have a good heart," he told her.

"Yes, and look where that got you now," she said before pulling the trigger four times in his face, then she put two more in his chest.

Seeing him dead made her smile. Now she could take over all of his operations. Rocky was making her a lot of money, but she didn't need him anymore. She wanted to run everything, so she cut him out of the picture. She left his apartment, walking towards the stairwell, when Wolf appeared with his gun out.

Boc! Boc! Boc! Boc! Boc! Boc!

A bullet hit Maryanna in the forearm, making her drop her weapon on the floor. Wolf saw her weapon fall and rushed towards her shooting, but she was faster. Maryanna dipped into a stairwell and jumped down a half flight of stairs. Bullets echoed through the staircase as she took off. Wolf saw she was already on the first floor, but he followed her outside. He was coming to kill Rocky, but when he saw his auntie, he knew it was now or never.

Outside, he saw she was long gone. He cursed himself out for missing his target. His auntie was becoming a big pain in the ass.

***

White Plains, NY

Keiline was asleep in her crib after the long day at a water park with her daughter. She woke up out of her sleep, looking to her right, thinking Wolf was there, but she forgot he told her he was going out. Normally her daughter would be hungry and want to eat around this time, so she got up to make a bottle. She heard a loud bang coming from a few doors down where her daughter slept. She rushed to the room to see four big men standing there waiting on her with guns out.

"Calm down," the Spanish man said, sitting down in a rocking chair next to the crib.

Keiline looked at her daughter to see her neck slit open with blood all over the crib.

"Ohhh my God, noooo!" she cried out.

"It's okay, young lady, better her than you," the man said.

Keiline fell on the floor in tears, crying her eyes out for the death of her seed.

"Let me tell you why this happened. I'm against killing kids, but you can thank Knight for this. Let me tell you a true story. Do you know how your father was killed? Your real dad, not your stepdad?" the man asked.

"You killed my daughter," she said.

"You still on that, young lady? We past that. But back to the story. Your dad was killed by Knight and Lil K's father, and now you rolling with them. That's dumb, but food for thought. I have to go. By the way, I'm Jose Martinez," he said, leaving the condo.

Keiline couldn't even look at her daughter, who was dead in a pool of her own blood.

Romell Tukes

Chapter 43
Long Island, NY

OG and Maryanna arrived at a nice, empty mansion they saw online, but they planned to purchase it. The area was a very upscale gated community and quiet.

"How's your arm, baby?" OG asked, looking at the Ace bandage on her forearm.

"It's okay. I can't believe I let that bastard shoot me," Maryanna said, taking a deep breath.

"It's okay. We gonna get him, trust me. That little nigga killed my son. If his mom was alive, I'd kill Rita too," OG said, thinking about his son CB who Wolf killed years ago.

"This is nice, papi," she said, getting out of the Bentley car.

"I like it. How you find this joint?" OG said as they walked inside the large mansion.

"I have my connects, baby. But speaking of connect, I'm glad you finally decided to give me your plug, daddy," she said.

"Yeah. I figured I won't be here forever so if anything was to ever happen, you will still be able to run the show," OG said, walking into the large kitchen.

"That was your worst mistake, papi," she said.

OG turned around, thinking he was hearing shit, but when he saw her gun in his face, his heart dropped.

"You on demon time," was all he could say.

"I been on demon time, boo. You was just too slow to catch on. I'm the one who gave you all them grimy ideas," she said.

It was her idea to rob Rocky and to kill her own nephew and other shady ideas. He only agreed with her because he was pussy whipped. What OG didn't know was Maryanna had been cheating on him for a while with other men - mainly his enemy.

"Fuck you, bitch! I gave you all my love and loyalty," OG shouted out.

"What the hell is going on with everybody screaming out all this loyalty shit? Y'all don't get it. Loyalty is only a word people use to sound good, but it can never exist!" she yelled, sick of people talking about loyalty.

"Do what you have to do."

"I plan to. We did have fun, but I put up with a lot of shit during these rough years for the blue faces," she said.

"You're a sack chaser."

"Clout chaser, I prefer to use," she said before pulling the trigger.

Bloc! Bloc! Bloc! Bloc! Bloc! Bloc! Bloc!

OG's body slumped into the counter and slowly slid on to the floor. Maryanna shook her head and walked out of the house she recently bought. Now she was headed to her new mission and everything was coming together.

***

South Bronx

J Balla snuck out of Sandview projects. He'd been getting money still lately with the little drugs he had left from Lil K's load. He'd been calling Lil K, but he changed his number. He felt something was up, but he couldn't pinpoint it.

Walking to his car, something stopped him. A red laser was to his head. Outta nowhere, ten red lasers pointed all over his body.

"I thought you was a solid nigga, son," a voice said.

J Balla looked around, but saw no one except lasers. Lil K appeared from behind two trucks.

"Lil K, what's going on?" J Balla played dumb.

"Do we really have to go there, bro? Your girlfriend Ari gave you up. You so dumb. She knew you had beef with Rocky, so to save her own ass, she gave you up. But she dead now."

J Balla wondered why he hadn't heard from Ari in a few days, but he thought she was mad at him.

"I'm sorry, bro. Rachela had me fucked up, K."

"I know, but it's cool, bro. We can't cry over spilled milk." Lil K turned to walk away.

"That's it?"

"Yeah. I mean, what else do you want me to say?" Lil K asked, looking in J Balla's eyes, knowing M Balla was turning in his grave.

Lil K walked off and Lil K's goons lit up J Balla's body with AR-15 bullets, leaving over sixty shells at the crime scene.

***

Yonkers, NY

Chills came down to the waterfront to see if he could catch Wolf coming or leaving. When he got the news of Rocky's death, he knew it had to be Wolf. One of Rocky's neighbors told him a woman got into a shootout at the same time Rocky died in the building hallway. He wanted Wolf's blood, so he planned to wait out here until he showed up to the condo he knew Wolf lived in at times.

His eyes started to close around 2 a.m. His passenger door opened and Wolf jumped in his car with a Glock 17 aimed at him. Chills couldn't even get to his weapon in his lap because Wolf took it.

"This is what happens when you cross sides, homie," Wolf said.

"You killed my brother." Chills looked at Wolf.

"So what? He was a snake and I ain't kill that fuck nigga. My daughter was just murdered, so I'm shedding blood all over the city until I feel happy again," Wolf stated, looking at him crazily.

Chills saw something in Wolf's eyes he'd never seen in any man's eyes. It was like Wolf turned into the devil himself.

Boom! Boom! Boom! Boom! Boom! Boom!

Wolf climbed out of the car and made his way back to his car, on his way to care for Keiline. Since losing his daughter, he'd lost his soul.

***

Knight flew back out to Miami earlier to meet up with Julie for a one on one. MeMe knew he was leaving NY to go to Miami and she was home in Costa Rica handling the new shipment. She was also feeling down because of the news of her murdered niece. Keiline told her everything Jose said and was shocked not only at the fact he killed her sister's daughter, but the news about their dad. Hearing that Knight's father killed their dad hit her hard. She didn't tell Knight yet and she didn't plan to. The only thing that really bothered her was what her sister said before hanging up. Keiline told her everybody would pay - including Knight.

***

Miami, FL

Coming back and forth to Miami was fun for most people, but for Knight, it was a headache. Julie asked him to come out so they could get some shit squared away. He told MeMe he was coming out and she was cool with it because she and Julie were on the same page now. With so much shit going on in New York, he didn't know if he was coming or going.

Last week, he saw J Balla's body on the news. He tried to reach out to Lil K, but he must have changed his number. Whenever Lil K got a new number, Knight always had it first and he didn't like that.

He parked the luxury rental across the street from a bar and restaurant establishment with a long line outside going almost around the corner. Knight had on an all-out clean Amiri outfit as he skipped the whole line entering the packed spot. There were so many beautiful women there. There was a sexy dark-skinned woman who almost made him forget he was in a relationship with MeMe.

Julie wasn't hard to find. She had the whole VIP section blocked off with her goons. He walked up to them and heard her voice.

"Move out his way," Julie said, sitting down with her legs crossed in a nice purple dress.

"Julie, how you been?"

"Alive."

"I see, but how's business?" he asked.

"Cut the bullshit. I called you out here to apologize for everything. I been hurt and lost since I lost my son and Kazzy," she said, drinking expensive champagne.

"No need to apologize."

"I had to. We have a big problem. Jose...he's not gonna stop until he gets us, him and his daughter. Unfortunately, the other little bitch dead," Julie said, wishing she would have at least seen Aliza die.

"I'm working on it, Julie."

"I have men in New York right now to help me and MeMe come up with a plan. Speaking of MeMe, what's up with you two?" Julie asked, being nosy.

"We're together."

"Like together-together?" she asked to make sure she heard clearly.

"Yeah."

"You don't think that's bad for business?" she asked.

"No and yes."

"Okay, I guess. A woman by the name of Marie came to see me to go against you."

"Marie?" Knight knew who it was: his ex-friend's wife.

"Yeah. I could have killed her, but it was bad timing. The owner of the place is a good friend of mine," she said.

A pretty white woman with a fat ass changed out Julie's bottles she'd pre-ordered.

"She is a problem."

"I know, Knight. But you letting NY go down the drain and you have to do something fast."

"I know," he said.

"Come on, I want to show you something Kazzy Loc left me." She stood up to leave and he followed.

Outside, cars and vans came from all directions and shooters jumped out with assault rifles. When they saw Rachela on one side and D Fatal Brim on the other, they knew it was about to get real.

Tat! Tat! Tat! Tat! Tat!

Julie got hit in her upper chest and her goons fired back with their semi-automatic weapons. Going against high powered rifles was no match, but they were fighting. Knight blocked Julie, shooting at Rachela and D Fatal Brim, who was gunning for him. People ran everywhere. Some ran into bullets. A Cadillac truck pulled up and Knight couldn't believe what he saw. Behadi and Lil K hopped out with the biggest assault rifles he'd ever seen.

Tat! Tat! Tat! Tat!

The noise sounded like thunder as Lil K killed four people in one spin. Behadi was dropping most of Rachela's and D Fatal Brim's goons. Seeing how they were now losing the shootout, Rachela took off and D Fatal Brim wasn't far behind her.

Knight looked at Julie who was laid out on the sidewalk unmoving. He picked her up and placed her in the Cadillac SUV that Lil K and Behadi were driving.

"Take her to a hospital!" Knight yelled.

Behadi peeled off.

"We was out here on vacation and saw you in that shootout, bro," Lil K said.

"I'm glad. Y'all saved the day," Knight said.

In the hospital, Julie ended up being okay. She had just blacked out after being shot.

Chapter 44
Glen Fuegos, Cuba

Jose Martinez was on his way to a business meeting in the next town over.

"Boss, something is wrong," the driver of his luxury car said as the car slowed down and went out. The car pulled over on the main street near a restaurant and bar on the block.

"There any gas in there?" Jose asked.

"Boss, I put gas in here earlier, I swear, but it's empty now," his driver said as the car went all the way off.

"Why is it on empty?" Jose asked.

"I put gas in there this morning."

"Oh yeah?" Jose pulled out his gun and fired two shots in his driver's head and told his security guard to leave the body on the side of the road.

Jose called for another ride, but a van pulled up and two sexy young women in skirts and heels got out. Jose didn't see their weapons until it was too late.

Boc! Boc! Boc! Boc!

The women fired over twenty-six shots into the luxury car. Jose was hit seven times, but was still breathing. When the car door opened, he was shocked to see his ex-girlfriend Maryanna there.

"I told you karma is real. I just robbed your spots, so I'm set for life. I had a feeling you were supplying OG, but it's over now," Maryanna said.

"Bitch," were Jose's last words before he died.

"I guess I am a bitch." Maryanna fired two more bullets in his face before leaving.

***

New York City, NY

Rachela rushed to the JFK airport to fly out to Cuba for the murder of Jose. She got the call two hours ago so she dropped everything to go home. Waiting for her flight, she had to piss, but her flight would be ready to take off in twelve minutes. She grabbed her purse and rushed to the restroom with no makeup on, so she tried to wear a hat to hide her zits.

***

MeMe had just come back from Costa Rica and she couldn't wait to see Knight. She heard what happened in Miami two weeks ago with him and Julie at the bar. Walking through the airport, she was surprised they let her pass with her pocket knife. MeMe saw a familiar face, but wasn't sure until she got closer.

"Oh my fucking God." MeMe followed the woman she knew was Rachela into the restroom area.

Her heart was racing as she slid into the restroom and locked the door. She waited on the sink for Rachela to be done urinating. When the stall door opened, MeMe attacked Rachela with her knife. Rachela tried to duck and sidestep, but MeMe was on her ass. MeMe was stabbing her in the head, neck, and face. Rachela fell hard from the vicious blows and MeMe stabbed her in the neck and heart over sixty times, killing her. MeMe left her dead body in the airport restroom.

Knight pulled up to pick her up out front. "You good, baby?" Knight saw blood all over her hand and shirt.

"Yes. Drive please."

"What happened?" Knight asked, pulling off in the Wraith.

"I killed Rachela."

"Oh," was all he said.

"Now let's take over the east coast, baby," she said.

"I'm with it, mami."

"Good, papi."

***

White Plains, NY
Five months later

162

D Fatal Brim and Marie had just delivered a seven-pound baby boy. They were in the hospital, overwhelmed with happiness. Marie wished she was in L.A., but D Fatal Brim was happy and had a few things going on in NY, so she didn't mind.

"I'm going to go get some juice, baby," he said, getting up to leave.

"Okay, get me some apple juice," she said, tired still from labor hours ago.

"Got you, baby." He walked out of the room.

He'd been trying to get ahold of Knight and Lil K. He hadn't been able to, but word in the streets was they had big things going on. He walked down the halls to see a man leaning on the wall.

"D Fatal Brim, congratulations on the baby boy," the man said, stopping him on his walk.

"Who are you?" D Fatal Brim looked at the man and realized who it was.

"I'm Wolf."

"I should kill you right here." D Fatal Brim's face tightened.

"Why do that if we have the same agenda and we could be useful to each other?" Wolf said.

"How? I don't really need you."

"That's where you wrong. We need each other and I got a plan to get Knight and Lil K and then take over the Bronx. Me and my girl Keiline will do this with or without you," Wolf said.

D Fatal Brim raised his eyebrows and smiled.

Romell Tukes

Chapter 45
Atlanta, GA
Months later

Knight had recently bought a mansion in the Buckhead section of Atlanta. He rarely came out here because he was so busy in New York, but when he got overwhelmed, he would fly out to the black Mecca. The mansion was 27,378 square feet, six bedrooms, four bathrooms, upper and lower level, four car garage, two pools in the back, two spacious living rooms, and a large kitchen area.

A few nights ago in the club, he met a few young Crips from the zone 3 area and they saw how he was shining and started to build with him. If a nigga ain't hear Knight's New York accent, then they would automatically think he was from the south because of his platinum teeth and long dreads.

He made a deal with a young nigga name Ropes, whose name was strong in the city. The deal was for Ropes to kill a man named Witty from East Atlanta, who was from New York, but had been getting money for D. Fatal Brim out there. Ropes knew Witty very well, so killing him was more of a pleasure than business because Witty killed one of his little homies a few months ago outside of a clothing store. Knight needed to expand a little, so opening shop in Atlanta was perfect. Even Lil K agreed with the plan.

Nowadays, Lil K was focused on his deen as a Muslim with Behadi, but he was still in the lifestyle. His little brother always talked about leaving the game alone, but Knight knew he couldn't. The reason why he knew Lil K couldn't was because they shed too much blood and tears to just give up and turn away, even though Knight had a few businesses like clubs, a warehouse, and a taxi service that were more than enough to go legit and never look back. The streets were in his heart and there was nothing he could do but accept his fate.

Life had been crazy for Knight. Losing his daughter, friends, family, and beefing with the Cubans was tearing his empire down. Now with him and MeMe in a relationship, it was making business a little easier. Lil K was controlling the drug transactions in the

Bronx with his own little crew. Since M Balla and J Balla, he was able to find a childhood friend's little brother to help move the keys around the city.

Since MeMe's sister Keiline and her boyfriend Wolf had been out of the picture since their child got killed, he didn't know what to expect or think. MeMe told him Keiline would never turn on her or betray her. They were sisters and blood. MeMe explained her sister was emotional and needed some time to clear her mind. Knight thought it was rare it took a person months to clear their mind, but he kept it to himself because he didn't wanna argue with MeMe.

Another issue was D Fatal Brim and Marie. The last thing he heard was he had been moving weight in Queens, Long Island and on the West Coast.

Knight cooked breakfast alone, listening to some slow jams, about to Facetime MeMe, who was on her vacation somewhere overseas.

***

Bronx, NY

Lil K cleaned and painted the mosque on Fordham Road. He came to this mosque to pray with the Muslims and attend Jummah.

"As-salaam-alaikum brother," an older man with a gray beard said, leaving the mosque.

"Wa laikum salaam," Lil K said as he climbed the ladder to paint the walls white. He had paint all over his face, body, and jumpsuit.

Lil K had been trying to become a better Muslim and his wife was trying her best to help him. Behadi was smart in religion. She knew the whole Qu'ran front and back. The only problem Lil K had deep down was he lived a double life and was one of the biggest drug dealers in the city. Every day he got in the deep thought of leaving the game alone and moving forward with his life on to something positive.

With thoughts like that, within seconds, demands came and ran those thoughts out of his head. Living and growing up in the nitty gritty south Bronx made it hard to break his ways of thinking because the street life built his mentality. Being married now and being alive made him open his eyes to more shit than he could imagine.

Beefing with the Cuban Cartel had to be the hardest encounter he ever had since going against Glock and his crew from Sandview. Jose Martinez and his daughters were running out killing shit with no type of mercy or sorrow. When Rachela's sister Aliza and him had sex the night he was drunk, he always wondered why she didn't kill him that night. Behadi found out and killed Aliza, but Behadi knew Lil K didn't mean to have sex with another woman. He was drunk and intoxicated. Her trust level went down for him, but in his eyes it made them stronger.

Lil K had a new operation in the Bronx because he was fucking with Lit Hound and his crew. Lil K saw a text from Behadi saying she was on her way.

Chapter 46
Bronx, NY

Behadi loved it when it was nice outside. It made the day a lot more enjoyable. She was bringing Lil K lunch and she wanted to speak to him, so she was on her way to the mosque. Seeing Lil K get more into his religion made her feel proud of him, but she knew at the drop of a dime shit could go left and he'd go backwards.

Living a normal lifestyle wasn't meant for her at all. Killing was second nature to her. Their beef with the Cubans died down so she had nothing to worry about besides a few nobodies.

In a couple of weeks she planned to take Lil K to Africa for his birthday week. She needed to go back home for a while because being in the Bronx was different energy.

Looking on the streets, she saw a bunch of young teens turned up trying to enjoy the summer vibes. As she stopped at a red light, her song came on Hot 97 the radio station and she turned it up.

A black Chevy with tinted black windows pulled up to the right side of her car. Behadi just so happened to look to her right to see D. Fatal Brim hanging out the window with a Mack 11 with a rabbit clip.

Tat. Tat. Tat. Tat. Tat. Tat.

Bullets from the submachine weapon busted out the windows. Behadi swerved around a public bus and got the fuck out of the trap area. Behadi drove up the block with a missing passenger window. The shattered glass was in her passenger seat and on her lap, so she couldn't move.

It didn't take long for her to get to Fordham Road, where Lil K was waiting for her outside the mosque. She parked in front of Lil K to see the crazy facial expression he had, but she didn't feel like getting into it.

"What the fuck happened?" Lil K said, looking at the Benz's windows busted out.

"Do you have to curse?"

"What happened? Are you okay?" he asked as she brushed glass off her lap and stood up.

Behadi wore a full body garment with a hijab to cover her face, as most Muslim women did. "I'm good, but here go your lunch. It's all Hala, babe." She opened the back door and handed him his container full of food that was still warm.

"You not going to tell me what happened, huh?"

"I hate when people ask the same shit." She got frustrated, forgetting she even had to speak to him about something.

"Damn, you leaving already?" he asked.

"I have to go get the window fixed. I'll see you at home," she said, getting back in the car.

Lil K knew she was also on her period, so he knew how Behadi got very cranky with an attitude. He saw her pull off and he went back into the mosque to finish painting.

***

Queens, NY

D. Fatal Brim was so mad that he just missed his target. He thought he had Behadi.

He had Queens and Long Island on lock with a few of his homies out here turned up. D. Fatal Brim and Marie had a baby boy and were doing well. She was back and forth to New York and L.A. while he was spending most of his time in New York.

He walked through Queensbridge Projects and saluted a few of his workers on his way to see Big O, his homie. Big O ran the largest projects in NYS.

The beef with Knight was still fresh on his mind. He wanted the Bronx and he planned to do whatever to get it. He respected how Knight crushed the Cubans, but he was coming harder and now with Wolf on his team, he planned to turn the city upside down.

Chapter 47
Turbo, Colombia

MeMe came out to visit her aunt in Turbo who ran her own drug operations, but there was a small problem at hand. The past few months, MeMe and her auntie had been using the same pipeline to get their product into the States. A few weeks back, MeMe's shipment was stolen and there were only two people who knew about the pipeline operation.

Knight and her auntie Sonfina were the only two people who had an understanding of what was going on. She asked Knight about it and he took her question to heart because he never betrayed anybody that didn't deserve it. MeMe came out to Colombia with some goons just in case shit got nasty because the Costa Ricans and the Colombians never saw eye to eye. Now that her auntie had taken over her late husband's cartel, she found it would be easy to talk to her.

Pulling up to the apartment building in the middle of the ghetto, she didn't like the looks of it.

"Park right here," she told her driver.

The two SUVs parked on the hill and she got out, looking at the blue building her aunt asked her to meet her at. MeMe had to leave her goons outside, which made her feel very uncomfortable. She walked up the stairs into the dirty building. The streets and building were both empty. Walking up to the second level, she saw two big Colombian men waiting on her with ear pieces and big guns.

"We have to pat you down," they said, patting her down to find two weapons on her.

MeMe was upset they got her guns, but she knew her auntie wasn't a threat. She was family.

"My beautiful MeMe," Sonfina said, turning around in a lovely flower dress. Sonfina was an older woman who still had some youth on her as she never aged.

"Hey auntie, good to see you," MeMe stated, sitting down.

"How's life? I heard you relocated to New York."

"Yes I have."

"Good. How's business? I'm sure you ain't come all the way out here to check on me," her auntie stated, staring into MeMe's eyes.

"I have something to talk about with you."

"Let me guess. You're speaking on the drugs that came up missing," Sonfina said with a smirk on her face.

"How did you know?" she replied.

"Long story, but to sum it all up for you, I have something to tell you," Sonfina stated as she looked behind her.

Keiline walked out in a short white Louis Vuitton dress, looking sexy.

When MeMe saw her sister walk out, her face flipped as well as her stomach.

"Look who it is," Keiline said.

"You steal my shit?" MeMe asked her sister.

"Stole? No, I took it, bitch. Any more questions?" Keiline shot back.

"You crossed your own blood," MeMe asked.

"Crossed?" Keiline posted up next to her aunty, who had set up this whole little reunion.

"Why are you doing this?" MeMe shouted.

"When Jose killed my son, he said it was because of Knight, so he will pay. I told you to pick a side and you chose dick, dumb bitch. Now look at you," Keiline stated.

"Knight had nothing to do with my nephew's death and you know that Keiline we were at war with the Cubans. You know that you just want someone to blame," MeMe said.

"MeMe, you never understood the value of family, just like your father, and now look at him," her aunt said.

"You won't get away. My men are waiting outside and y'all got thirty seconds before they run up in here," MeMe said.

"I hate to tell you, but your goons are on my payroll now. The only reason why they ain't kill you yet is because I wanted to do it myself," Keiline stated, sitting down and crossing her legs.

"You gonna let this old bitch brainwash you?" MeMe asked.

"Old?" Sonfina took it offensive, ready to kill MeMe herself.

"This is bigger than Sonfina, She just helped me bait you." Keiline had her gun ready and loaded.

MeMe saw Sonfina's head get blown off as bullets from another building ripped through her aunt's body. The sniper on a roof nearby also shot the two guards in the room.

Tat. Tat. Tat. Tat.

Keiline knew she had to get the fuck outta there as bullets tore the building up. MeMe saw her sister aim her weapon at her until Knight ran in the room. Keiline let off a few shots at Knight before she took off downstairs and out the back.

"You good?" Knight said, helping MeMe off the floor as she was surprised to see him.

"Knight, what the fuck are you doing here?" MeMe asked as they walked outside. MeMe knew Keiline was long gone, so chasing after her was pointless in her mind.

"I know something wasn't right when you told me your shit was robbed. Once you told me about Sonfina, I did my research and I knew it was her, so I followed you out here. Plus Behadi needed a vacation," Knight looked outside to see all of MeMe's security guards dead on the street.

"Behadi!" MeMe was happy to see her friend.

"Hey MeMe," Behadi said with a big-ass military rifle in her hands.

"Y'all saved me," MeMe said, smiling.

"You slipping," Knight said.

"I know. It won't happen again."

MeMe looked at her goons on the floor and knew if it wasn't for Knight and Behadi, she would be done. She was mad her sister got away, but she wouldn't be hard to find. Wherever Wolf was at, then Keiline would be close. She knew that for a fact.

Chapter 48
Yonkers, NY

Dalia encircled his cock with both hands and began stroking it slowly from the base to the head. She sucked up a large droplet of precum that oozed out the slit.

"Shit," he moaned as she continued to work his magic stick slowly, deliberately frustrating Drake's desire to cum.

His hands fondled her big tits and then made his way to her thick brown thighs and fingered her wet crotch. Dalia stopped sucking his penis so he wouldn't climax even though she was eager to swallow his entire load. She positioned herself in his lap on his king-sized bed since she was nice and wet.

"Fuck me, babe," she said as he slid inside her tightness.

Once he got her open, she wasted no time in bouncing up and down, feeling his shaft inside of her. She was on the verge of a serious climax when he held her in position as he started to pound her pussy out. He began to grunt before he exploded in her pussy.

Drake's phone going off fucked up her vibe and her nut as he pulled out.

"Oh my fucking God!" she shouted as he got out of the bed ass naked to answer the phone.

Dalia was a beautiful brown woman with thick thighs, phat ass, flat stomach, big tits, tats all over her body, and short hair that suited her. She was classy and eye candy. The two had been together for some years now and she had plans on marrying him one day. The only pause was that he was deep in the street and she was a probation officer.

"Baby, I have to go," Drake said, getting dressed.

"Oh really?" She caught an attitude, looking at Drake, who had the body of a god. He was light brown with dreads, handsome, and his body drove women crazy. He was a winner.

"Don't do that, ma. I'll be back in a few hours. It's only 8 p.m.," he said.

"Well, I'll be asleep so don't wake me up, fuck boy." She hid under the covers.

"What I told you about that?" he said, putting on his Rolex watch, in a rush to go meet his plug.

"Since you came home from the feds, you changed. When I was coming up to PA to visit you every week, you sold me sweet dreams," she said.

"How did I do that if I'm here with you?" Drake said.

"Whatever, boy, bye," she said.

Drake shook his head, leaving his crib, going out the front door.

***

Drake drove his Range Rover to the library near the metro north train station. Driving through Yonkers, he saw a bunch of young teens out there selling drugs on street corners. He knew the young cats should be home asleep or getting ready for school. Drake knew most likely the drugs floating through Yonkers were from him and his crew.

Growing up was rough for him because he was raised by his grandma. His mom and dad both went to prison for drugs and both got sentenced to life imprisonment – at least, that's what his grandma told him. He had no choice but to fend for himself. Drake gained respect in the streets from robbing to selling dope in his hood, Riverdale.

Drake got caught in a forty-seven man federal indictment and was sentenced to eight years in federal prison. He did most of his time in PA, mostly USP's, which is a high-level maximum security prison. When he came out a few months ago, he met his plug in a clothing store. Drake went to the cash register and couldn't afford a Nike Tech sweatsuit and his plug popped up outta nowhere and bought him $10,000 worth of clothes that day. Drake didn't even know the man until later on that day when he saw him again at a corner store. After his first shipment, he built his own foundation in Westchester County and never looked back.

Pulling up to the library, he saw a black Ferrari parked in the lot.

Jack Boys vs Dope Boys

***

Wolf saw Drake's Range Rover and jumped out, happy to see his worker he took a liking to. Wolf had been dropping off so many bricks to Drake on the daily basis he got overwhelmed, but he had been knocking them off.

"What's the vibes?" Wolf said.

"Some shit," Drake replied.

"What's been going on with the city?" Wolf hadn't been in town in a month.

"A couple of minor setbacks. The police raided one of my spots, but I got it under control," Drake stated, leaning on his car hood.

"Copy. But when you gonna be ready for me?" Wolf asked.

"This weekend. I still got a few keys left and gotta pick up some money."

"Don't worry about that. You good, br. I'ma have it for you on Friday, but that Bronx nigga gonna drop it off," Wolf stated.

"Who? D Fatal Brim?"

"Yeah, he family."

"He's vibes are funny, son, but I do it for you, brotty." Drake didn't like D Fatal Brim because he tried to raise the set price on Drake so he didn't respect it.

Romell Tukes

Chapter 49
Lower East Side, NY

Wolf drove back to his condo downtown that had an amazing view over the city skyline. Moving downtown was great for him because the city was so big it would be hard for any opps to catch him and Keiline.

His girl Keiline told him she'd be back in a few days. Wolf had no clue where she was at and he didn't like to question her because he felt like he could trust her. Losing a child was the hardest thing he had to swallow since losing his sister. Every day he thought about his dad, Ryan passing, his brothers, his sister, his mom, and now his dead child.

When Keiline came up with the decision to go against MeMe and Knight, he had no choice but to be on her side and support her choice. It was kinda hard for him to go against Knight because he liked the kid's vibes and loyalty. He never crossed anybody close to him so this didn't feel right to him, but he knew deep down it was Knight's fault his seed was dead. Seeing Keiline backstab her own sister, he prayed she wouldn't do him the same way one day.

Wolf still had Yonkers in a chokehold with the drug game thanks to Drake. Unlike TT and Chills, he planned to keep Drake out of any beef he had because losing money again wasn't worth the beef.

The long haul issue he had with OG didn't last long because his time out from jail was short-lived thanks to Maryanna. Wolf's aunt Maryanna was out for self. He had no clue she was so crazy and vicious when she used to train him as a kid. He hadn't heard from her in some time now so that was perfect. He hadn't even heard from Knight or his crew, but he knew they were lurking somewhere in the Bronx.

Parking in the garage area, he took an elevator upstairs to his condo. Wolf saw flowers with a note attached to it and brought it inside. Once inside, he read the note out loud.

"Hey Wolf, this is your aunt Maryanna. I'm back, I'm sure I'll be seeing you soon. Sorry for the loss of your baby. You can always make another one."

Wolf couldn't believe what he just read. He was very upset and all he could do was sit down.

***

Long Island, NY

Lil K heard Behadi get out of the shower and he waited for her to talk, but she walked to her walk-in closet and acted as if he wasn't there. Lil K loved Behadi. She was a bad, sexy woman without makeup. Lil K loved his black women. They did something to his soul and body.

"Behadi?" he yelled, getting no type of reply.

"Stop calling me," she stated, walking out in her gown.

"What?"

"You deaf now," she shot back.

"Behadi, we need to talk. You my wife, baby, and I don't want to lose you, baby," he said.

"Lose me?"

"Yeah. We been going back and forth and I don't want no smoke. We got enough on our plate," Lil K said.

"You got some growing up to do," she said.

"I just want you to leave the game alone," Lil K said.

"You leave the game alone, and get the fuck out my bed," she said, kicking him hard and making him fall out of the bed.

"You got it, ma." Lil K left the room, controlling his anger.

Chapter 50
Harlem, NY

Maryanna had recently bought a brownstone apartment building she now owned and rented to civilians. She controlled most of Harlem drug trade now since she took Rocky and OG Chuck out of the picture.

Maryanna sat Indian style on her couch, watching the Oxygen channel on TV, chilling, getting a peace of mind. Lately she had been worried about Wolf and what he had up his sleeve because just a few months ago, she was trying to kill him.

Maryanna was selfish and only cared for herself. She wanted Yonkers to herself, but she knew Wolf wasn't trying to share and that was a big problem. Raising Wolf to be a trained killer was her goal when he was young so he could come work for her one day, but her plan backfired. A long time ago Maryanna had a secret only a few knew about, and that was her son she had with a man she didn't even know on a one night stand when she came out to New York. Every day she thought about her son, whom she only saw a few times because she chose it to be this way. She knew sooner or later it would be almost time to reach out to her son. Growing up rough, she knew it wasn't smart or honorable to raise a kid in the same atmosphere.

Maryanna felt her eyes closing so she went to the room and went to sleep dreaming about taking over New York, but she knew she wouldn't be able to do it alone.

***

Pelham, Bronx

Lil K drove to the graveyard to see his ex, Red, the woman he still loved until this day even though she was dead. He wished he would've never showed her the game because she let the game eat her alive. Once she got shot and lost her memory, he thought she would want to get out of the game and start a new life. Instead, she turned into a gorilla and she became worse to the point where there was no controlling her.

The night she killed herself, his life changed in so many ways. He thought he would never be able to move on. When he started dealing with Behadi, she helped him emotionally and mentally. Without her, he would've had to check into a mental house. Behadi even knew how sensitive he was about Red and that's why she was in the passenger seat of the Lambo SUV.

"I'm with you," she said, rubbing his hand.

"It's cool, ma. I'm just placing some flowers on her grave for her birthday," Lil K said, pulling up to the long pathway leading up towards some graves on the hill.

"She's in a better place now, babe. You did all you could to save her," Behadi said.

"I know."

"Stop being hard on yourself," she said.

"I'll be right back." He parked the SUV and grabbed the flowers out of Behadi's lap, leaving her one on top of her beautiful dress.

"Take your time," Behadi stated.

Lil K took his time walking up to Red's grave. This was his second time coming to her gravesite and every time he came, he had tears in his eyes.

It was a nice day out and Red's grave had a fresh set of flowers as if someone had just placed them on her grave. He added his flowers to her grave and stood there for a half hour reminiscing.

***

Rikers Island Jail, NY

Riker's was the worst county jail in the state of New York's Justice Department. The jail had different buildings with sections for different gang members and mental health patients.

Izzy Balla's name was heavy in the four buildings where he had lived for the last three years fighting three murders he was accused for outside of a Queens club. At twenty-one years old, all he knew

Romell Tukes

was jail and surviving in the Bronx streets. He was from one of the roughest projects in the city. His grandma raised him and his sister since they were kids because both of his parents were junkies. A while back when Izzy was selling rocks to eat, he shot his father by mistake because he was smoked out and unrecognizable. His mom had been back and forth to jail and rehab since he was a baby.

Izzy was born in a drug treatment program. He was the true definition of a crack baby. His sister was a year younger than him and doing well selling houses. She was the only one there for him. She went to visit him and held him down financially. He came to jail with a gang of women, but when they saw him and his boy Lit Hound on the news for three murders, they all left.

Izzy was a pretty boy, a short, light-skinned nigga with colorful eyes that drove the women crazy. His friend Lit Hound was able to make bail, but Izzy was denied bail because of his record. Lit Hound paid for his lawyer, but that was all. He hadn't seen him since court, but his trial was in a few weeks so their fate would be made.

Izzy Balla did pushups in his cell, thinking about court and becoming a Muslim like Lit Hound, but he was too much of a Blood to study religion, in his mind.

Chapter 51
North Miami, FL

Julie spent the weekend at her condo to prepare for her meeting in Cuba tomorrow. Her security team was on standby, waiting for her go signal. After the death of Jose Martinez, a new cartel family took over Cuba and formed an alliance with Julie. This was the first time in history she ever did this because the beef between Julie and the Cubans had been going on for years. She knew the Cubans couldn't be trusted at all, but a truce wouldn't hurt. She and Knight were cool now after a long rocky haul since knowing each other.

Julie had a new issue: people trying to take over Miami. Stephen was one of her main rivals right now and her people had been going back and forth with her over turf. After losing her son, she started to develop flaws that were new to her, like sniffing coke on the regular and worrying too much.

In front of her was a glass table with coke scattered around in lines. She felt like she had nothing to lose anymore, so using drugs took her to a place that felt so good she wished she could never leave.

After sniffing two more thick lines, she went to take a shower and tried to take a nap, but the coke had her geeking so she couldn't sleep. She'd been losing weight and that nice frame she used to have was now gone, but she knew plastic surgery was always an option.

***

Uptown, Bronx

Lit Hound climbed out of the drop top coupe, dripping in designer gear with two choker chains on, stunting on the block. RPT projects had a one way in and one way out entrance for visitors and people who lived there. He wasn't from there, but he had a few workers who locked down the projects. Since he came home from his murder cases on bail, he'd been focused on getting to a bag and paying off his lawyer fees and Izzy Balla's lawyer fees also.

He was originally from the Millbrook projects. He had known Lil K for a long time since he was a little bad-ass kid. Getting money wasn't anything new to him. He started scamming with his crew of Bloods. Growing up in the Bronx in a gang-infested area, he got into a gang called Blood Hounds who were into everything. At twenty years old he was about his bread and getting running through the streets.

"Yero, where this nigga Poor Boy at, son?" Lit Hound asked Twin.

He was always posted up in his wheelchair in front of the building. Twin got shot up by the police a few years ago and now he had to use a wheelchair for the rest of his life. The good thing about his situation was he had a big lawsuit with the city NYPD for shooting him eight times in his lower back.

"He inside, yo. But what's the vibe? You coming out here like you can't get jacked." Twin joked a lot.

"Nigga, you know how I give it up. I'll have your ass rolling down the block ass naked," Lit Hound shot back, seeing the upset look on Twin's face.

"You always take jokes too fucking far, fam," Twin said before rolling off in his wheelchair, getting emotional.

A few chicks came out of the building and Poor Boy came out behind them, rolling up a blunt while walking. He was an ugly, black nigga who always dressed poorly to throw people off, but he was really getting real money. Before linking up with his boy Lit Hound, who was in the same set as him, he was robbing shit in other cities like Queens and Harlem.

"What's shaking, bro?" Poor Boy said, throwing up his gang set with Lit Hound checking out his attire.

"You ready for dem joints to land?" Lit Hound referred to bricks of coke as joints.

"I been ready, nigga," Poor Boy said as seven niggas came out to chill in front of the building.

"Say less. I'm just stopping by."

"What's going on with that case?" Poor Boy asked, knowing he was out on bail for some serious shit.

"I go to trial soon so I'm just trying to make sure my funds are right."

"I feel you, son. Izzy Balla still on the Island?" Poor Boy asked.

"Yeah, he chilling."

"Shit be litty on da rock. My little nigga just got clapped," Poor Boy said, smoking his blunt.

"Damn, son, I be knowing how shit be. I cut two niggas while I was up there," Lit Hound stated.

"I'm throwing a party in a few days for my birthday in Brooklyn with da homies. Come out to show some support." Poor Boy's birthday was this weekend, and he didn't go out much so he planned to turn up.

"You remember what happened at the last club party?"

"This ain't that, son. You and Izzy Balla was odee wilding," Poor Boy said, remembering the night they killed all dem people outside the club.

"I'ma sleep on it. I gotta slide, so text me later. I have to go to New Jersey."

"A'ight, I got you, bro."

Lit Hound climbed back in his drop top and raced off, bypassing a few thots. He loved to show off and be flashy. He was that type.

Romell Tukes

Chapter 52
Los Angeles, CA

Marie loved her West Hollywood mansion. It was her safe haven when she came home to Cali. Being in New York so much, she forgot about the west coast. She still had L.A. under her wings dealing with the Mexican gangs and the Black Hounds. Her husband, D Fatal Brim, was still in New York, but he still had the Crips and Bloods in L.A. moving their product. Since having a child, she had changed in a short period of time. Marie became insecure about herself and developed new emotional traits. The thing she feared was her husband and baby father mistreating her after having his child, as most males did to their baby mothers. To her surprise, D Fatal Brim still treated her like a queen, even better than he did before the birth of their child.

The doorbell woke her up out of her sleep. Marie climbed out of bed with her morning face. She looked good in the morning without makeup. She was all natural. Throwing on her robe, she put her pistol in her robe pocket because she ain't trust nobody.

D Fatal Brim had their child in New York. She took a two-day vacation from them, but Marie really missed them both. She made her way downstairs to see a man with flowers standing on the other side of the glass door. She thought her husband was the one who sent her flowers because he did little things like this.

"Thank you, who are these from?" she asked, staring at the colorful flowers while seeing the man reach in his lower back.

She saw the name Knight on the paper and automatically she went for her weapon.

Boc. Boc. Boc. Boc.

Marie sent rounds into the delivery man's head, killing him, then she looked around to make sure nobody was lurking around the house.

"Fucking bitch!" she yelled, running upstairs to pack her shit so she could leave.

Knight found out where she lived and she knew spending another minute here was too deadly. So she packed up and took an

Uber to the LAX airport, heading to New York. The only thing on Marie's mind was to kill Knight and everything he loved. She was glad her baby was with her husband or that could've been bad.

Teaming up with Wolf and Keiline was a good idea, but she knew nobody could be trusted, especially a chick who was willing to turn on her blood sister.

***

South Bronx, NY

Janet Mildred was a beautiful, slim, flawless, dark-skinned woman with a natural look and smile. At twenty-one years old, she was fresh on the police force and she had one main goal, and that was to ruin Knight's life.

Janet was Valentine's little sister who was off in college in Texas when she was alive and dealing with Knight when Valentine started work on the force. When Valentine and her niece Karmala got killed, she blamed Knight for it because Valentine was a good girl until she met Knight.

Janet and her sister both grew up in the Bronx and always wanted a better way out, so they got educated and went to college to become police. Becoming a cop was big for her because she saw so many of her black people get harassed, shot, or killed by the same people who were supposed to protect and serve. She would fool anyone with her sexy look and her innocent ways, but Janet had serious mental issues since she was a kid.

Growing up with a serious case of bipolar she learned she also had a split personality which landed her in a mental hospital once when she was sixteen for a little over six months. Outside looking in, she was perfect, but within she was dark and soulless. Janet wanted to fuck up Knight's life because she loved her sister. She was the only person who fully understood her, and Knight helped take that away. Valentine and her talked all the time about Knight when Valentine moved to Chicago and Texas.

She was in her apartment getting ready for work, but she had to stop to take her medication.

Chapter 53
Dominican República

Stephen laid on her upper deck getting a tan as her yacht cruised the ocean between Haiti and D.R. She owned the 197-foot yacht with rooms, a kitchen, bar, and three levels to enjoy the ocean. Three of her goons posted up on the lower level, playing cards for money. Stephen needed a break from Miami because the beef between her and Julie was getting outta hand. A lot of her people were either getting killed in the war or going to prison.

Last week twenty-two of her workers got snatched up by the feds and half of them were ratting on her. She had a black book with all of her workers' family members just in case shit like this happened. Being a boss bitch comes with a lot of headaches and stress.

Outside looking in, she made shit look sweet and easy, but that was a show because for the love of riches, shit got tense. Coming from VA then to D.C., she learned a lot, especially from her brother Gotti, who was murdered a while back. Even though she and Gotti didn't see eye to eye, she still looked up to him and took game from him. When she came to Miami, her life changed. She found opportunity and a chance to elevate her foundation. That was years ago. Now she was one of the biggest queen pins in the south. She had a lot of clients, but there was one she couldn't get her mind off of.

That one client was Knight. He was that one person that brought happiness and satisfaction to her. Whenever she thought about him, sparks would fly from her head. Their relationship sexually didn't last long, but it was the best sex she ever had. Since Knight, there were many men after him but none could ever compare to him, even her new boo. The last she heard about Knight was that he killed the Martinez Cartel from Cuba whom she hated, especially Rachela's hoe ass.

Stephen would pop in and out of the States daily. She never stayed in one spot for too long. She learned the game early, so she believed in the motto outta sight outta mind.

***

Yonkers, NY

Drake sped down the Cross County Expressway to meet Wolf at the Cross County movie theater. Shit had been getting real nasty in his neighborhood. Five of his workers got caught up in three different raids the same night at different locales. Something wasn't right. He had a strong feeling someone close to him was talking to the police.

Being from the streets, it wasn't hard to put shit together. Since dealing with Wolf, he had been flooding his whole county with keys from Yonkers all the way up to Brewster, NY. Besides the streets stressing him out, he had other problems. He was beefing with his girlfriend over a social media post. Drake didn't have time for dumb shit. He was trying to win. He had everything in front of him: a plug, a crew, hoods under his control and money.

The big BMW spaceship pulled into the lot and it wasn't hard to find Wolf's car. He brought out an all-white Wraith.

"Big homie." Drake hopped out with his chains hanging.

"Drake, my guy, good to see you," Wolf stated, embracing him. Wolf liked Drake a lot. He was young and ambitious.

"Out here trying to get it."

"True. What's going on in the city? I don't be in Yonkers too much because I don't be moving like that anymore. I got a little older and I got a lot more to risk now," Wolf stated.

"I feel you, brody, but shit looking really spooky out here," Drake said.

"What you mean by that? You look like you eating good and you starting to cop so much weight I'ma have to have my men make two trips," Wolf joked, but he was serious also.

"The police raided a few of my spots and got a couple of my little niggas off the street. I think it's a little more to it though," Drake stated.

"You think or you know?"

"I gotta do my research, but I'ma handle it," Drake assured him.

"How many bricks are left?" Wolf asked because he had a stash waiting for him at a storage center.

"Sixty-five or some shit."

"Okay, when you get to your last twenty, come see me."

"Copy, bro," Drake said, leaving.

Romell Tukes

Chapter 54
Manhattan, NY

Lil K was waiting in the DMV line to renew his license, then he had to go meet up with Lit Hound. To his surprise, his boy was doing numbers and he was making a killing. Having Lit Hound on the team was like having a J Balla and an M Balla built into one, so having him was a big plus.

Behadi had been on her best behavior. He was planning her a big trip for her birthday. It took another thirty minutes for him to be seen. After paying two hundred dollars to renew his license, he slid through the crowd and made his exit.

Outside, he walked with his head down reading some papers he had just got, but then he bumped into a woman he almost knocked over.

"Oh shit, mami, sorry," Lil K said, looking at the sexy Latina woman, but when he looked at her harder, he then reached for his gun.

The woman smiled when she saw him reach for his gun. "There are four cops sitting behind us, so if you not trying to die right here, don't do it," she said with a smile.

"I'ma kill you, Maryanna."

"I know. I hear you and Knight don't deal with each other?" Maryanna asked.

"He's dead too."

"That's good to know, handsome," Maryanna told him.

"I guess I'll see you sooner rather than later," Lil K told her.

"You will honey," she said before walking off into the DMV.

Lil K looked at the four cops parked up across the street eyeing him, but the whole time they were looking at Maryanna.

He couldn't believe he just ran into an opp. He hated Maryanna and Wolf. He wished the cops weren't there. He would have killed her in broad daylight.

***
Gun hill Projects, Bronx

Lit Hound pulled outta the jets on his way to meet his big homie Lil K. It was early in the afternoon, but Lit Hound had to speak to Lil K and then he had to go see his lawyer downtown. His court date had been stressing him out because he knew if he was to blow trial he could spend the rest of his life in jail. Being signed to the streets was not as hard and crazy as it seemed, but you did take big risks of going to prison or death.

Lit Hound's girl was blowing his phone up because he didn't go home last night and she was waiting on him. He spent the night at Izzy Balla's girl's crib. He had been fucking her since he came home on bail. Lit Hound knew it was fucked up to fuck his boy's girl, but she threw the pussy at him and she was a bad bitch, so he couldn't help himself. She caught him one night coming out of a club drunk and since then he had been hitting her. The pussy was so good it made it hard for him to turn away now.

Driving through the Bronx with a bag full of money in the truck, he knew if he got pulled over there was a chance he could go to jail and get his money snatched. It didn't take long for him to get to his location, which was a lot next to a highway. The vacated lot was in between two buildings. Lit Hound's main thing was stacking money and lawyer fees. He wanted to make sure his lawyer was paid and full. Luckily, he and Izzy Balla had the same lawyer so that made it a little easy for Lit Hound to keep tabs on Izzy Balla. When he paid for his lawyer, Lit Hound only paid for Izzy Balla's fees because he didn't want him to snitch on him. A lot of times when niggas got locked up with serious cases, the police will try to get them to turn state and flip. He knew Izzy was a solid nigga, but he understood solid niggas fold too under pressure.

Lil K pulled up and got out of the truck, grabbing the bag of money he owed Lil K. "What's the vibes?" Lit Hound embraced Lil K, handing him the bag, taking a peek down the street to make sure the coast was clear.

"I just ran into this bitch I should've killed, but the time was fucked up." Lil K rubbed his beard he had been growing out, which was a part of his religion in Islam.

"Who?" Lit Hound knew from the grapevine in the streets that Lil K and Knight had some serious beef in the streets. Lit Hound told Lil K a long time ago his beef became his beef.

"Maryanna. She the nigga from Yonkers auntie. His name is Wolf," Lil K said.

"I heard of him, bro."

"Facts. But fuck dat, what's going on with you?"

"I'm about to go see my lawyer."

"Oh yeah, I forgot about that case, bro. Leave it in Allah's hands." Lil K got real religious on him real quick.

"Always. But that's the money I owe you. I'm ready for you whenever you ready to drop that load off," Lit Hound stated.

"Gotcha." Lil K checked his watch, realizing he had to go.

"I gotta slide." Lit Hound said the same thing that was on his mind.

"Be safe."

"Big facts, son."

Romell Tukes

Chapter 55
Camaguey, Cuba

Julie walked into the nice hotel/resort in Cuba next to a small river. The small city was a tourist spot so there were a high traffic area filled with drug selling and prostitution. The two men she brought with her opened the doors for her, walking through the lobby on her way to the back outside restaurant area. The hotel had an outdoor kitchen and restaurant for their guests. It was very classy and nice for a vacation.

Walking out back, she saw a gang of security guards surrounding the man she came to see. Sama smiled at her, waving to her to come over and have a seat.

"Sama, hey." Julie put on her best smile because the day could go good or bad in a matter of seconds.

"Julie, you look beautiful," he said, looking at her Fendi white dress.

"Thanks. I see you ordered some food," she said, seeing pork, chicken, fish, beans, rice, and Spanish food in front of her on the table.

"Yes, enjoy, dig in," Sama said as he started to eat.

Sama was the new boss in Cuba since Jose Martinez got killed. He had spent years as the real underboss climbing the ladder. When he got the news of Jose and his vicious daughter's deaths, he had a big party. Jose never really liked Sama because he fucked one of his bitches. Jose knew better than to cross the line because Sama was an official killer just like his dad, who was a legend in Cuba for over a hundred killings. Now with Cuba under his belt, he was the man of the year and he didn't play no games when it came to his country.

"Thanks for calling me. I haven't been to Cuba in a long time," Julie said, eating some of the food.

"That's because you came out here to my country on bullshit and tried to kill everybody," he joked.

"The issue with Rachela and Jose was getting outta hand and you know my track record dealing with the Cubans," she told the truth.

"I know. So why are you really here today? Because I know your type that can't be trusted. I heard a lot about you, Julie, and that makes me nervous." Sama stared at her.

"Never was I the perfect woman, but I did what I had to do to survive. I just want a truce with you and to start this relationship on a new level. There's no need for us to have issues from our past," she said.

"Spoken like a true lady."

"As always," she blushed.

"I have people in Miami, but I'm running into a roadblock in your city and I may need some help with this one individual named–
—"

"Stephen," she finished his sentence, already knowing Stephen was a headache.

"How did you know?" He had a surprised look on his face.

"That bitch in the way. I'm eliminating her in due time." Julie's statement was bold.

"We on the same page."

"I agree," she said, grabbing her drink from the table.

"Hold on, don't drink that." He stopped her.

"Why?"

"I put a sleeper in your drink just in case you came on some bullshit and tried to manipulate me, but everything you say, I see you're sincere about it, so you have my blessings and helping hand," Sama told her.

"Thank you. I'm sure I'll be in touch soon," she said.

"Okay, please do. I like your presence," he flirted.

"Trust me, old man, I'm too much for you," she said, getting up to leave.

***

Manhattan, NY

Knight chilled in his office in the back of his nightclub, waiting on MeMe to arrive. He still had a few businesses, but the club was doing the best. Going into business with a Jewish man was one of the smartest ideas he came up with in a while.

Looking on top of his desk he saw the Noble Qu'ran and opened it to chapter 49 and started to read. He was never really into religion, but seeing his little brother and Behadi on their deen heavy made him wonder if he was missing something. Knight also felt like he was missing something very important in his life. The more he read, the more he started to think that Allah was the missing piece to his life. With so much going on in his life, it seemed like a movie and ten years ago, he would never imagine living life at this level.

Romell Tukes

Chapter 56
Manhattan, NY

MeMe climbed out of her all-white Jaguar coupe in a short dress and heels, looking like eye candy. It was six o'clock in the afternoon and the club only had a few staff working. She liked the club set up. It had flashing lights above her head, two bars, two dance floors, a lower level, and a large DJ booth. An hour ago, she texted Knight and he told her he was at the club getting some things in order with the pay stubs. She wanted to come by and spend some time with her boo.

They both lived two different lives. In their relationship, she was a plug and he was a client and a hustler running a few legit businesses.

"Hey babe." She walked inside his office to see him reading a book.

"Hi, good to see you." He got up to hug her and kiss her soft, sweet lips.

He knew MeMe was always on the run nowadays back and forth to Costa Rica to New York. Any time with her, he made sure to cherish it and spend it with her. Having a woman like MeMe in his life was amazing. She made life seem so carefree and joyful. If a person were to see MeMe, they would have no clue she was one of the biggest drug dealers on earth.

"What you reading, one of them books by Romell Tukes again?" she asked, because she had caught him reading the *Gangster Qu'ran* and the *Killers on Elm Street* series by the author Romell Tukes a few times.

"It's the Noble Qu'ran. I think Lil K left it here," he said.

"That's for the Muslims?" she said, sitting in his lap.

"What you know about that?" he asked.

"I know the Muslims. Behadi taught me some things like who Allah is and she had me thinking… Papi, you know my whole family is Catholic, but she made good sense, daddy." She opened the Qu'ran and read it.

"So you want to become a Muslim?"

"I didn't say that, but I wouldn't mind learning the religion," she made clear to him.

"Okay, that's good, baby. But how's shit looking in Costa Rica?"

"Good, good."

"That's all?"

"I mean, business gonna always be business, daddy you know how this shit goes."

"You been hanging around me too much, baby, you starting to talk and sound like me. You don't even got no Spanish accent no more. You sound like a Bronx bitch," he joked.

"Shut up," she laughed.

"Let's go out to dinner, baby." Knight knew she deserved a night out and to be treated like the queen she was.

"How about first we make love?" she said, going for his belt buckle.

She didn't even give him time to reply as she pulled out his hardened penis. MeMe moved her thong under her dress to the side and he entered her wetness slowly.

"Ohhh shit, daddy," she moaned out loud, slowly grinding his pipe.

They fucked for over an hour on the floor, table, couch, and in the chair over and over.

***

New York City, NY

Lit Hound walked into his lawyer's office to see him talking on his cell phone. Lit Hound had been waiting in the lobby for over an hour to speak to his lawyer about his case.

"You done yet?" he asked rudely.

"I'm sorry, Mr. Steven, I had a very important call," his lawyer, Mr. Sweeney, stated seriously.

"What's going on? You ain't been answering my phone calls."
Lit Hound looked into the white man's eyes, seeing him look
through papers.

"I'm sorry, I had so many damn cases."

"What does that have to do with me?" Lit Hound asked.

"I know you have a court date soon and I spoke to your co-
defendant," Mr. Sweeney said.

"What's the D.A. talking about and what's our chances of
beating the case?"

"60/40 chance."

"You sure?"

"Yes, I'm positive," Mr. Sweeney said.

"We got two weeks from now right?" Lit Hound asked.

"Yes, and we get to pick the jury. It will be six women and six
males," the lawyer said.

"Okay, I'm ready," Lit Hound said, getting up.

"Good luck."

"I don't need luck. I need you to beat this shit like OJ." Lit
Hound laughed, leaving.

Romell Tukes

Chapter 57
East Atlanta, GA

Witty drove to his dad's crib for Sunday dinner. His dad was a preacher in a church. He and his dad had a good relationship. At first their bond was on the edge because his dad didn't like him selling drugs or hurting people. Witty was from Brooklyn, New York, but he'd been living in Atlanta for the past couple of years running up a big bag. Coming to the A from Brooklyn, he brought his New York swag down there and he got in touch with his boy D Fatal Brim that he was in the feds with.

D Fatal Brim came to the city and they met up at a hookah bar. Since that day, D Fatal Brim had been supplying him work by the boatload. He had goons all over East Atlanta and they were all Bloods under him. He was a sex, money, and murder gangbanger.

Pulling down his dad's block, he saw his truck parked out front, so he knew his dad was there. Witty parked in his dad's driveway next to his truck. He climbed out and walked inside the crib.

"Pops!" he yelled out, walking into the house he was able to purchase for him.

Witty's father had been in Atlanta for over twenty plus years and his mom lived in New York. Growing up in BK was rough, but he was able to survive and bring his hustle to Atlanta.

"Pops!" he yelled out again and walked into the living room.

Witty walked into the dining room to see his dad's head busted open as he was laid back in his chair.

"Fuck!" Witty reached for the gun he thought he had on his hip but forgot in the car.

"Witty," a voice said, coming out from the kitchen.

Witty turned around to see Ropes and four soldiers standing there.

"Hoe-ass nigga." Witty knew he was finished.

"You talk a good one," Ropes said.

"Fuck you, son, you know how my niggas coming!" Witty shouted.

"It's too late for that," Ropes said, aiming his Glock 17 handgun to Witty's head.

Boc. Boc. Boc. Boc. Boc.

Ropes and his Crips left the crib after they trashed the place to make it look like a robbery. On his way to Zone 3, he texted Knight, letting him know everything was a go.

Taking over East Atlanta wouldn't be a hard thing because Ropes had a few Crip homies over there on standby. He had some people from Flatbush in Brooklyn and they spoke highly of Knight saying he used to be out there and how heavy his name was in the city. With Knight on his team, Ropes knew he could take over Atlanta. He already had his section in a chokehold.

***

Barahana, Dominican Republic

Maryanna and a van full of goons drove through the Barahana Hills on their way to visit one of her old friends. When Maryanna was introduced to the game at an early age, it wasn't by OG Chuck. Her godfather Wee showed her the ropes and the ups and the downs to the games when she was twelve. Wee showed her how to shoot, kill, package tons of kilos, and how to run a business. Growing up under a man like Wee, she learned a lot, but the main thing she took from him was how to be a double-headed snake.

She knew Wee had been out of the game for close to twenty years and she heard he was doing bad, living in a small house in the ghetto of Barahana. Needing a break from New York, she took a trip back home to D.R., the country she loved to death.

Two Bentley trucks pulled up in a rundown neighborhood to see little kids running around looking for a meal. She walked out of the SUV in heels looking like a diva. She walked in the small house to see Wee sitting on the floor reading a book in Spanish about a British fighter.

Wee was a very old man with a gray beard. He spoke good English and Spanish. Back in the 60s, 70s, and 80s, he ran a pipeline to D.R., to New York and other countries. Now he had nothing to stand on or to cherish. Other cartel families killed his children so he had nothing.

"Maryanna," Wee said, putting on his glasses to make sure it was her. He hadn't seen her in over ten years, but he heard she was doing well and he felt proud.

"Wee, nice to see you," she shot back, looking to see old food on the floor along with rats, maggots, and flying roaches. She felt disgusted standing there but she had come to ask him a question.

"You look great. Give your godfather a hug." He stood up.

"No. You think I don't remember what you used to do to me at night? All the times you fucking raped me," she said, seeing his face scrunch up.

"Maryanna."

"Don't, please. I came to ask you about a man named Knight. He had a father who used to run with you," Maryanna said.

"I know who you're referring to. I've been hearing a lot about him. His dad was a part of my crew until he killed my wife and brother," Wee said sadly.

"What do you know about him?"

"Trust me, Maryanna, this man is very different, but word is he's dead."

"Do you believe so?" she asked.

"Me?"

"Yes. Be honest."

"I don't know, but if he's not then anybody who harms his children has a better chance of killing their own family as well as themselves," he said seriously.

"How did he die?"

"I heard many stories, but if he is alive, then you will eventually know," Wee told her as he picked up a rat from off the floor as if it were a pet.

"Okay, do you know his name?"

"Shadow or The Darkness. He goes by both, but I think he's gone. A lot of powerful people wanted him dead and they say Jose Martinez killed him."

"That's hard to believe," she stated.

"I agree."

"Nice seeing you, but I have to go." She dug in her purse, pulling out a gun. Wee's eyes widened.

Boc. Boc. Boc. Boc. Boc. Boc.

"Creep."

Maryanna stared at his dead body as the rats bum rushed Wee's flesh. She thought about all the times he raped her as a kid. She'd been living with the pain since then.

Chapter 58
Bronx, NY

Today was Lit Hound's court date. It was trial day and he wore a nice, clean, gray Armani suit with his Rolex and diamond bracelet. He walked into the busy Bronx courthouse, ready for his big day. He was nervous and had bubble guts. This morning he took five shits. He had bags under his eyes because he hasn't slept in days waiting for this special day. He had enough money put up for commissary and to play with that would last him a lifetime if he had to do a long bid. He saw his lawyer talking to a tall white man with a bald head on the second level.

"Mr. Sweeney." Lit Hound caught his attention as his lawyer finished his convo.

"I'm glad you're here. We're next. I just spoke to the D.A. and they on some all the way shit, bud, so we gotta fight hard. I don't want you or your co-defendant to take the stand because it will fuck up what I got going on in my cross examination with a few of the new witnesses," Mr. Sweeney said, checking the time.

"I trust you."

"I hope so. Come on, it's time." Mr. Sweeney walked into courtroom seven, his lucky number.

Lit Hound saw Izzy Balla's girl and his sisters as well as other supporters for Izzy Balla. Izzy Balla's girl tried her best not to make eye contact with Lit Hound, but she couldn't help it. Izzy Ball looked back in his Cartier frames, peeped the vibe, but he brushed it off as Lit Hound made his way to be seated next to him.

"Nice fit, son," Izzy Ball stated.

"I see you, bro, but let's beat this shit," Lit Hound said, seeing the judge come out.

"Facts, blood," Izzy Balla said as he rose.

The trial lasted a few hours and Sweeney did a hell of a job at cross examining the witnesses who came to trial, but they had different stories, so that fucked up the D.A.'s testimony who was going off the witnesses he found. The judge was confused that the

D.A. didn't have anything solid enough to make the jury or judge even side with him.

"This is a serious triple homicide and you have nothing solid we can use to convict these two gentlemen." The judge looked at the D.A., whose face turned fire red.

"Judge, this must be a mistake. I thought my witnesses were going to be able to carry on with their statements on the stand," the D.A. said.

"A mistake, huh?" The judge shook his head.

"Yes."

"Well, your mistake got these two gentlemen acquitted. This case is a wrap. Sorry for the inconvenience, gentlemen. Case dismissed." The judge stood up, going to the back.

Lit Hound hugged his lawyer while Izzy Balla had tears in his eyes. He thought he would be going away for the rest of his life like a few brothers he met on Rikers Island.

***

Manhattan NY

Izzy had just pulled his penis out of his girl Jamara's wet pussy in an expensive hotel room she got for the weekend for him.

"You good, ma?" Izzy could tell there was something wrong with her.

"I got something to tell you," she said, sitting at the edge of the bed covering her big breasts with the bed sheets. The bedroom had a Jacuzzi inside with a good view of the Hudson River and New Jersey.

"Not right now, baby girl. Come give me some of that fire head." Izzy laid on his back, ready for action.

"Izzy, I really gotta tell you this," she cried.

When he saw the tears, he knew she was serious. He'd known her for years, since they were kids. She was his first love and they had a solid relationship. Being locked up, Izzy knew she would roam and get her rocks off, but as long as she kept it classy, he was cool with it. At first in the cell it used to stress him out but then a nigga named Coach told him a bitch gonna fuck regardless and the more a nigga pressed her about it, the more she would eventually do.

"What's up?"

"I'm pregnant." She had real tears rolling down her face because she really loved Izzy.

"You pregnant by who? You violated, son." Izzy jumped up.

"Lit Hound," She cried harder.

"What da bro gotta do with this?"

"It's his baby and I'm keeping it, Izzy." Jamara had her head down until he slapped her so hard she fell off the bed.

"Fuck you and that nigga! Bitch, you lucky I won't kill your dumb ass." He got dressed and left the hotel room.

Jamara stayed on the floor crying and screaming, knowing it was only the beginning to his madness.

Romell Tukes

Chapter 59
Long Island, NY

Knight came out to L.I. to check in with his boy Gucci, who he knew from the Bronx, but was getting money in Hempstead, L.I. now. Last week Gucci contacted Knight and asked him to meet him as soon as possible because he had something to tell him in private. He hated coming out to L.I. There were too many bad memories. The club he had in L.I. he recently closed to focus on his Manhattan club that he had the Jewish man he went into business with run.

MeMe had just left for Costa Rica this morning, so he had a week for himself and to break down the new load of coke he got yesterday. When MeMe came around, he knew hustling was over until she went out of town because she wanted all his time for herself. MeMe loved to lay around the crib and make love all day. Knight loved to fuck also, but he wasn't as crazy as MeMe was with it. She could go all day and all night.

He met Gucci where he requested, which was in a recording studio in Hempstead, a small section of L.I. that was ghetto. Knight had seen Gucci come up in the rap game. He'd been seeing him in local rap artist videos and he heard a few of his songs on the radio. He brought out his Bentley today because it was a beautiful day. Parking next to a white Yukon SUV, he saw Gucci and two of his boys come out of the small studio connected to a barber shop.

"Knight!" Gucci yelled, smiling at the man he used to look up to growing up.

Gucci was from Millbrook PJs but when he got arrested for a gun charge and caught a four year bid, he started to rap. When he came home from upstate prison, he started moving weight to get studio time.

"I see you out here." Knight saw Gucci's diamond chain and bust down Rolex watch he had on.

"This my first advance. You know I had to bust it down, bro," Gucci said, flexing his watch.

"I see. But what's da vibes out here? It sounded like you wanted me to pull on some emergency shit," Knight said, seeing Gucci's facial expression change as he looked over Knight's shoulder.

Knight could tell something wasn't right by the looks on Gucci's face so he turned around to see four men creeping behind him a few feet. Knight tossed his hands in the air, looking at a familiar face.

"Finally got you, son." D Fatal Brim smiled with a Glock 17 with a 30 shot clip in his hand.

"Welcome back," Knight said.

"I been back, homie. I was just waiting on my time, son and today is my time, boy." D Fatal Brim was face to face with his ex-best friend he'd known since he was a kid.

"Why you back dooring me, outta all people? I know it's not that Mexican pussy?" Knight could tell he hit a vein talking about his wife Marie.

"You got a real slick mouth, playboy, but I'ma shut it today, fam. But to answer your first question, I was always loyal to you, bro, and when I went to jail, you carried me like a sucker nigga because I was down bad," D Fatal Brim said. "Nigga, I was there for you." Knight stated facts, knowing D Fatal Brim had other shady reasons.

"Man, I called you to kill dis nigga and y'all having a fucking reunion," Gucci said, wishing D Fatal Brim would hurry up and kill Knight.

Gucci had heard Knight and his crew killed his older cousin, Pop Off, a few years back and he wanted blood. When Gucci got wind that D Fatal Brim was looking for Knight, he linked up with him to set Knight up.

D Fatal Brim looked at Gucci and fired four shots in his chest as his crew ran off back into the studio.

"Back to you, hoe nigga. I'ma kill you and take over the Bronx, so I guess you a big dub now," D Fatal Brim said, lifting his gun.

Shots went off, but it wasn't from his weapon. D Fatal Brim saw his men dropping as he turned around, seeing somebody was sniping his goons out. Knight grabbed his gun and pulled the trigger at his face, but it jammed. Bullets were going wild. Knight and D Fatal Brim took cover as they ran in different directions. When Knight got to his car, he saw Lil K and Behadi pulling off. He had them come for back up because he knew Gucci was Pop Off's cousin and he also heard Gucci was selling for D Fatal Brim, so Knight tried to set up his own trap that had just backfired.

Romell Tukes

Chapter 60
Edgewater, NJ

Stephen wore a white Chanel dress with a white pea coat, looking out towards the city of New Jersey in her high-rise condo. She had two guards waiting outside her apartment at all times to protect her from any enemies or anybody thinking about trying her. Relocating to Jersey was something she had in mind for a long time, but she was so stuck in Miami and the DMV area she didn't have time to move around. Her main reason for being in Jersey was to get closer to New York so she could try to work her way in. She knew New York was Knight's turf, but since she knew Knight wasn't trying to share, she planned to squeeze her way into his city by choice or force. When she was doing business with him, she had no clue it would eventually turn sexual. Men like him were hard to come across, but she wished their relationship could have stayed on the business level. When he started dealing with Julie, her rival and competition, she grew some type of hatred and evil in her heart towards him. It would have been too easy for her to send some goons to kill him. She'd rather hit him another way: his pockets.

She took a sip of her expensive wine and took a deep breath, thinking about how she conquered Miami and soon New York would be next. She already had a few people in New Jersey moving weight for her, but nothing was like that New York money.

***

Midtown, NY

Behadi and MeMe decided it would be cool to go out for lunch in the upper-class section of the city. MeMe had just gotten back in town and she had to check on some things back home. MeMe had been having problems with getting drugs to Brazil because the police kept interfering with her shipments, basically stealing, and she was upset. Running the type of business she did, stealing was the ultimate death no matter who did it, when, why, or where. She had an understanding with the Brazilians and they had agreements with the police so the drugs could easily come in with no issues. She had a feeling there was a little something more to what she was told because a few tons were taken from a location only two other people knew about.

"You look stressed," Behadi said.

"Oh, me?" MeMe shot back.

"Yeah, you." Behadi ate her fancy stew, which she wasn't liking.

"I just been thinking about giving this life up and starting a new life." MeMe got serious.

"And do what, MeMe? You run a very powerful organization. You can't just wake up one morning and say okay, I want to be a regular person." Behadi looked around at all the uppity white folks in their fancy suits laughing and joking without a care in the world.

"I want to settle down, Behadi. I'm still young and beautiful. I want a family of my own and a husband. I had a crazy life, but I don't think I'm meant to grow old in this lifestyle." MeMe's Spanish accent kicked in.

"You have to follow your heart and do what's best for you," Behadi told her, understanding.

"You right."

"What did Knight say?"

"I haven't spoken to him. We both so fucking busy. Whenever I'm up here, I want to just spend time with him," MeMe said.

"I feel you on that, but I think he will understand."

"I hope so, but he gets his work from me, so if I tell him I quit, then what if he don't want to?" MeMe asked.

"Sometimes you have to live for yourself," Behadi said.

They enjoyed their evening together and got their nails and hair done up.

***

Yonkers, NY

Drake and Wolf stood outside a truck company late at night in the cut. The police didn't come around this section at nighttime because nothing was going on. They were surrounded by old, abandoned factories and warehouses. This is where Wolf felt comfortable doing his drug transactions with Drake.

"This will make us even," Drake said, passing him two heavy duffle bags full of money in rubber bands.

Drake had been doing his thing in his city but also he'd been getting money in the little town outside of Yonkers. He was on his way to locking down all of Westchester County real soon.

"Yeah, we straight. I must say I'm proud of you." Wolf tossed the money in his BMW, waiting on his people to come in an SUV with the drugs for Drake.

"Thanks to you."

"You putting in your own work out here in these streets," Wolf told him.

"I'm just trying to get to a bag, bro," Drake said before seeing a pair of headlights coming their way.

As the headlights grew closer, Wolf realized it wasn't the SUV his men were supposed to arrive in.

"You know them, son?" Wolf's words were cut short when the van doors flew open and four men hopped out with military style assault rifles.

Tat. Tat. Tat. Tat. Tat. Tat. Tat.

Wolf saw a bullet hit Drake in his legs, but that didn't stop either one of them from shooting back.

Boc. Boc. Boc.

Bloc. Bloc .Bloc.

Drake caught one of the gunmen with a nice headshot. Wolf shot one in his chest making him spin backwards before falling. Wolf took cover, trying to make sure Drake was good, but he was busy firing at the gunmen.

Boc. Boc. Boc. Boc. Boc. Boc. Boc. Boc.

Drake and Wolf worked together and hit the last two men standing. Wolf knew the goons sent at them were rookies or else they didn't know how to use an assault rifle.

"One still alive," Drake said, limping to the gunman who was still moving.

They got up on the gunman and kicked him in his nuts.

"Ahhhhhhhhh!" the Dominican man cried in pain.

"Who you work for?" Drake asked.

"Maryanna! Maryanna, she loco," the man stated, thinking the men would spare his life.

Bloc. Bloc.

Wolf shot him in his head and saw his goons pulling up a short time later in an SUV filled with drugs.

"That's them?" Drake said, holding his wounded leg.

"Yep, I just hired them both," Wolf said as the two young men approached. They were smiling until they saw the dead bodies on the ground.

"It's all here, boss," one of Wolf's foot soldiers stated before he saw Wolf lift his weapon.

Bloc. Bloc. Bloc. Bloc.

Wolf fired shots into both men's upper bodies and climbed in his BMW, looking at Drake.

"Have someone get your car from down here quickly and take the SUV full of drugs. Clean up your cut. Sometimes in life you have to take some to give some, fam," Wolf said, looking at the bloodstain on Drake's Amiri jeans.

"I know how it goes," Drake said as he pulled out his phone and called his boy Frazier to come pick up his car and take it to Riverdale.

Wolf couldn't believe Maryanna got up close on him. He felt like he was slipping now.

What Wolf didn't see was the all-black Audi coupe that had been parked in the cut, watching his every move for the past few days or so.

Chapter 61
Los Angeles, CA

Knight, Lil K, and Behadi all landed in the LAX airport from their long flight. Knight figured they could all use a weekend getaway, so he had Lil K leave Lit Hound in control of all their product. At first Lil K thought trusting Lit Hound with all the products would be a risk, but Knight told him to give dude a chance.

"I'm so tired," Behadi said, following Lil K and Knight out of the airport, cranky because she was on her period and very moody. Behadi needed a little get away, so this was perfect for her, and she loved the City of Angels.

"The way you was snoring, I can't see you for being tired," Lil K said because he was unable to sleep since leaving New York due to her loud snores.

"Shut up," she laughed.

"What's the plan?" Knight asked as he saw the Rolls Royce limousine parked in the front awaiting them.

"Shopping," Behadi said first.

"I got something lined up for you, ma," Lil K told her as she stopped and looked at him.

"What's that? I don't like surprises, you know that," she said with an attitude.

"A day at the spa and a shopping spree." Lil K handed her an envelope filled with money and tickets for the spa resort she had to be at in a few minutes.

"Ohhh, thanks babe." She gave him a hug, kissing him, and he gave Knight a wink.

Lil K was trying to ditch Behadi so he and Knight could go handle some business in Compton.

"No problem, baby, you deserve it," Lil K said, opening the door for her as Knight shook his head with a smirk.

"What's so funny, Knight? And why y'all not getting in?" Behadi asked, seeing they weren't getting the limousine.

"This is for you, babe. Today is your day. Me and Knight gonna chill at the hotel until you're done enjoying your day."

"You sure? I feel like something is up," Behadi looked back at Lil K and Knight, trying to read them both.

"Girl, go enjoy your day," Knight said, closing the limousine door on her.

"You know I'm gonna hear about this all day," Lil K said, realizing Behadi had his gun in her bag. They took a private jet so they could fly out to L.A. with their guns.

"You will be good. Let's go pick up this rental car."

They took a cab to a rental spot and got a Mustang GT35 to ride around in.

***

Compton, L.A.

Driving through Compton was like reliving the movie *Boyz N Da Hood*. There were houses close together with weights in the front yard and old school cars hooked up parked in the front.

"This shit look like some shit off a movie," Lil K said, seeing niggas posted up with blue flags on one block then red flags a few blocks down.

"Nigga, these niggas banging for real out here. I just hope this shit goes well," Knight said, looking for Spruce Street.

"I think this nigga solid. Shit, he hit me up on IG explaining the situation with D Fatal Brim," Lil K said.

Two weeks ago a man who went by the name Big Ru hit Lil K up, telling him about a man named D Fatal Brim. Not wanting to talk too much on social media, he told Big Ru he would holla at him in person.

"This is it," Knight said, pulling over in front of a big house on the corner surrounded by goons dripping red flags.

Before even getting all the way out of the car, six men approached them to make sure they weren't the Fruit Town Brim or rolling 60 Crips because it was on sight beef with the gangs.

"Ayyy, where y'all from, Blood?" a tall, skinny kid asked.

"New York," Knight said, walking towards them.

"New York? What set y'all claiming, homie? Y'all better not be that 9 Trey shit but we fuck with them Sex, Money, Murder niggas," a fat nigga said, blowing weed smoke in the air.

"We ain't banging, son. We here to see Big Ru," Lil K said.

"Well how come y'all ain't say that? Follow me," the tall skinny kid said, taking them to the backyard area where loud music from a rapper named Mozzy was being played.

It wasn't hard for them to find out who Big Ru was. He was the loudest and biggest nigga in the place.

"Aye Big Ru!" the tall kid yelled to get his big homie's attention.

Big Ru was an ex-con who was a Piru gang member with his own set. He had just come home from doing ten years in jail on his third bid. He stood 6'7" and weighed three hundred and twenty pounds. He was also part of the Black Guerilla Family that was big in the Cali jail system and streets.

"You Lil K?" Big Ru's voice was deep and stern.

"Yeah, and this is my brother Knight," Lil K said, introducing Knight as Big Ru looked at them both.

"Everybody go inside," Big Ru told his goons.

Once the backyard was clear, Big Ru pulled out a 40 ounce of Old English to drink to the head.

"Thanks for reaching out to us, son," Knight said, sitting down.

"My little homie Cory speaks highly of you." Big Ru looked at Knight.

"Cory from the Bronx?" Knight knew a Cory from Hunts Point in the Bronx who moved out of the city years ago with the feds raiding his block.

"Yeah, he's part owner of a car wash with me. He like family to me, so that's how I heard about our similar situations dealing with this D Fatal Brim character," Big Ru said, taking a sip of his beer.

"What he do to you?" Lil K asked, trying to see his angle.

"D Fatal Brim been supplying my opps and he had my little brother killed by The Ave, a Mexican crew across town," Big Ru said, frowning his face upside down at the thought of his little brother's death.

"He got some people out here in L.A.?" Lil K asked, already knowing the answer to his own question.

"Yeah, him and his bitch," Big Ru said.

"His bitch got some pull out here, huh?" Knight asked.

"Hell yeah! She got mostly every Mexican and Crip out here under her wing," Big Ru told them.

"Can you help us get at them?" Lil K asked.

"Yeah. It's gonna take time because I heard they be around your way now," Big Ru said.

"We know, but we gonna stay in touch," Knight said, forming a quick plan, but he knew it had to be planned out fully first.

Chapter 62
Hollywood, L.A.

Behadi was in the spa getting pampered, thinking about childhood. Having to kill her family made her heart turn colder than ice, but now being in a relationship with Lil K made her soften up. She felt like something was wrong with Lil K or like he and Knight were up to something.

She saw a gang of Korean women posted up massaging and giving out hot oil treatments to clients. She needed this meditation day because lately she felt depressed.

After close to two hours of getting herself together and all types of treatment she was ready to do. On her way out, she saw a familiar face surrounded by four big Mexican men with mean faces.

***

Marie sat in a chair with her eyes closed, getting her feet and legs rubbed.

Boc. Boc. Boc. Boc. Boc. Boc. Boc.

When Marie heard the gun sound, she jumped up and started to take cover, especially when she saw her guards go down. Marie looked right into Behadi's eyes and got the fuck outta there, leaving her goons to get killed.

Korean women ran and yelled, hoping not to get hit. Behadi saw Marie jet out the back and knew there was no point in trying to chase her. Behadi ran out the front into the crazy commotion going on outside as police cars arrived. She tried to blend in with the crowd and she made it to the limousine.

"You okay?" the driver said, pulling off.

"Yeah, some crazy white man just went crazy in there shooting people," Behadi said in a panicked voice.

"Oh my, white people are acting a fool out here," the older black driver said.

***

South Bronx, NY

It was 10 p.m. Lit Hound had ten keys of coke in his white BMW M8. Driving down Clay Avenue, he was on his way to drop off the work and pick up some money from KJ, his worker. He'd been trying to reach Izzy Balla so he could hit his hand with some money and coke so he could get on his feet. When Lit Hound came home from the Island, he was down bad on his knuckles, so he knew his boy needed him. Jamara hadn't called his phone since Izzy had been free so he was glad she was playing her position now.

He made a quick left and saw police lights flash behind him.

"Fuck!" he shouted, pulling over, not trying to go for a chase with ten keys and a pistol in the back with a thirty shot clip.

When he parked, he got his ID license and registration, ready for the bullshit. The only thing he feared was police trying to kill him like they did two of his cousins last year. The thing about the NYPD was most of them were crooked and criminal minded so if they wanted you, then they would eventually get you.

"Excuse me, sir, you forgot to put your blinker on," Officer Mildred said at the window.

Lit Hound knew the beautiful dark-skinned woman from somewhere but it didn't click because he never saw a cop so sexy.

"I'm sorry, I must have been speeding," Lit Hound responded, looking at her badge and name.

"Let's cut the bullshit, Lit Hound. I know who the fuck you are and I know you got some shit in the trunk and I know who you work for," she said with a serious face.

"If you think you know all that, then why the fuck you just stop me?"

"I have my reasons," she smirked.

"Do what you have to do because I ain't no snitch," Lit Hound said.

"I know that, but I'm just saying hi to you."

"I don't know what types of games you playing, but I'm a South Bronx nigga. We get to the point, no capping or beating around the bush, cutie," he shot back.

"I'll see you again, and you're still the same cocky bastard," Officer Mildred said while walking off.

Lit Hound looked in his driver's side mirror at her nice ass, thinking about what she meant by her last comment.

***

Queens NY

"Queens get the money!" Big O shouted while shooting dice in the back of 40 projects with a crew of young boys, going crazy over the dice game with $170,000 on the floor. All the big time drug dealers were shooting dice putting on a show but some of them were waiting for the right time to walk off while Big O was busting their heads.

Big O was getting so much money. He was trying to lock down every projects in Queens, but the only problem was he gained a lot of enemies over the years. Niggas hated him with a passion, but they feared him too much to do any harmful thing to him because he had some hitters.

While shooting the red dice and talking shit, Big didn't see a man in a red hoodie walk through the crowd with a gun out. When a few people saw this, they got the fuck out of the man's way. The crowd got quiet and Big O was the only man talking. He looked up to see Izzy Balla aiming a gun at him.

Boom! Boom!

Big O's brains landed all over the money.

"Let niggas know Izzy Balla from the Bronx did this, you heard! This nigga a rat. He wrote statements on me," Izzy Balla said, pulling out the paperwork. He handed it to one of the witnesses, who was scared to death, before walking off.

Romell Tukes

Chapter 63
Manhattan, NY
Days later

Knight had been back from his L.A. trip for a few hours and he was already planning a kill attack for his ex-friend D Fatal Brim. Meeting Big Ru was a blessing because he knew D Fatal Brim was back and forth to New York and L.A. now.

When Behadi told him she ran into Marie at the spa, he couldn't believe her luck. Behadi told him about the shootout and how she missed her target. Knight couldn't believe it because her gun game was on point.

MeMe was already at the condo when he arrived and she was more than happy to see him. She had the shower running while he laid in the bed, thinking about all of his past enemies, from Glock to Fats, and the list went on. Seconds later, MeMe came out of the bathroom dripping wet naked with a pair of Chanel heels on.

"Stand up, papi, and give me what I been missing," she said, walking toward him, licking her phat lips, ready for what the night had in store.

Knight loved her sexy, curvy body and the way her phat pussy poked out like a kneecap. MeMe got on her knees, slowly savoring his cock while twisting her head slowly as if she was making out with his penis.

"You missed me, papi?" she moaned, deep throating every inch.

He leaned back, watching his cock disappear into the back of her throat. The loud noise of slurping could be heard as she picked up the pace until she felt his climax hit the back of her throat. After licking her lips, she stroked his cock and positioned herself on his lap, ready to ride.

"You trying to drain me today," he said, gripping her waist as he worked his way into her tight hole.

When he got her loose, it was on and popping. His thrusts got stronger and fast, making her beg and scream for more. He sucked on her nipples, making his tongue swirl around her hard nipple.

"Ohhh yesss," she growled, biting her lips as he stroked her pussy with deep strokes, making her climax.

Her pussy was now dripping. She couldn't believe the mind-blowing orgasm she just had. MeMe wanted to give him another blow job because she knew he loved it. She made her way to his shaft and slowly inched downward, breathing through her nose before savoring his rod until it reached the curve of her throat. When her lips made it to the base, she paused and gradually slid back up.

"Goddamn!" Knight yelled. His toes curled as she made his pole wetter with her saliva before quickly swallowing his length again, now bobbing up and down. He couldn't take it anymore and spurted a hot load of thick cum into her mouth.

She swallowed every drop and then he returned the favor, eating her good-tasting sex box. They fucked and sucked like two teens in heat all night.

***

Harlem, NY

Wolf had a little two-bedroom brownstone uptown in Harlem World in a middle class neighborhood. He was in the steaming shower when he heard the bathroom door open. He had his pistol on the sink just in case.

"Babe, that's you?" he said. He heard nothing while trying to get a good look through the foggy glass window.

The shower opened and Keiline stepped in naked, gripping his cock with no talking as she got on her knees and forced his dick down her throat. She gagged a little while making loud noises as she got wetter. Before he could cum in her mouth, she stopped and bent over, holding on to the cold and hot water knobs. Wolf was so horny he felt like his penis would snap any second. His cock made contact with her cunt, which was warm and gushy. Entering her doggy style, she went forward as he slow-fucked her.

"Damn, daddy," she cried.

Keiline started throwing it back on the dick once she got adjusted to his length. Her juices poured onto his rod as his hips thrusted deep into her slit. Her pussy tightened around his cock every time his dick slammed inside of her. Wolf loved the way her ass jiggled with every pound. Both of their breathing got quicker and heavier while he thrust into her cunt faster.

"Fuck me harder!" she shouted at the top of her lungs, urging him to go deeper inside of her.

He spread her ass cheeks and went wild inside of her, pounding her back out. He held onto her hips, pressing it down, so she couldn't run from the pleasure. Wolf slid his dick into her asshole, which was so tight the tip couldn't fit back there. Wolf pulled out and ate her ass out for a minute, then he slid back in the back door, making her cry in pain and pleasure. When he made it halfway in, she stopped him because it was too painful, so she sucked him off and went for round two in the room.

Chapter 64
South Bronx, NY

It'd been a week since Izzy Balla killed his big homie Big O, and the streets were asking questions.

Izzy's mind was now focused on money so he could get to a bag, so he came out to Webster Projects to speak to his cousin Rosa Balla, who was in the same gang as him. Izzy knew his cousin's projects were known for getting money, so if he could find a plug to rob and feed the pj's, he'd be on.

Izzy couldn't shake the thought of how his best friend, Lit Hound, did him. He never knew it was fake love, but he did know when he saw him it was lit. Catching a case with a nigga meant everything, especially when niggas kept it solid, but when a person crossed the line, that bond is tossed out the window. Now Izzy's mind frame was to get it out of the mud and build his own crew from the ground up, then go to war with Lit Hound and whoever he was running with.

Walking into the projects filled with skyrise buildings, he saw a couple of dudes outside he knew and gave them a light head nod. Rosa Balla lived in the back. When he got to his building, he walked in the lobby and outta nowhere, he was ambushed by sixty Bloods with guns and Rosa was in the front.

"Sorry cuz, but you violated. Big O was a big homie, the big Mack, bro, and you fucked up," Rosa Balla said.

"Nigga, you and Big O can suck my dick!" Izzy shouted showing no signs of fear because he knew today was his last day on earth.

Rosa Balla was about to punch the man in his face until he heard the lobby door open and saw a familiar face. Izzy Balla paid no attention to the man behind him as he thought about how grimy his cousin was for setting him up. Izzy knew Big O was connected, but not to the whole city of New York.

"I got him, sleeze," a voice said as everybody turned around to see that it was the big homie of the whole state and set.

"Who da fuck are you?" Izzy Balla asked.

"D Fatal Brim, homie. Take a walk wit' me. You owe me. Big O was my worker but now you killed him and you his replacement, scrap."

"What? I don't owe you shit," Izzy replied.

"Fuck dis nigga, we don't need him," Rosa Balla said before D Fatal Brim blew his brains out for talking outta turn and setting up his own blood.

"Take a walk wit' me," D Fatal Brim said as he walked out of the project building.

Izzy looked at the goons surrounding his cousin's dead body, shocked D Fatal Brim just killed his cousin, and he was lost. Thinking how his cousin just tried to set him up, he would've put two bullets in him himself. The name D Fatal Brim was heavy all over because he and Knight were legends in the Bronx so whatever he wanted with him, Izzy knew it had to be big.

Izzy followed the big homie outside and climbed in an all-red new Bentley GT coupe.

***

Eastside, NY

Maryanna was asleep in one of her condos, fresh from her trip. Trying to focus on a bag, her opps, and staying alive was more stressful than being in Iraq with an American flag tied around your head. In a few days she had to go out to Texas, but before then, she had a drop on Wolf and one of his trusted soldiers who was moving through Yonkers, NY.

While sleeping in her gown she thought she was dreaming when she felt something enter her pussy hole. She jumped up, but a punch to her face knocked her back down. She saw a man dressed in all-black. He had a barrel to a sawed-off pump stuffed in her pussy.

"Move again, bitch, and I'll blow this shit the fuck off now listen to me clearly. I hear you been looking for me?" the man said in a deep, strong voice.

"Who are you?" Maryanna couldn't see the man because the room was too dark.

"We'll get to that. I came back to the States for two reasons. Don't make it three. First, my daughter Angie was kidnapped in Miami. She is only eighteen years old. A cartel family took her. Have you heard anything about it?" the man asked.

"No, I swear."

"I'm also here for my sons Knight and Lil K. If any harm comes to them, I'll kill you," the man stated.

"You're Knight's father? I thought you were dead?"

"I won't get into that. I'm back and there will be a lot of blood to pay if I don't find my daughter, and you're going to help. I'll give you a few days to get yourself together." The man left her condo as smoothly as he came in.

Maryanna panicked. She couldn't believe what just happened. She knew there was a choice to make. She had beef with Knight and his crew also so this could turn out bad either way. Never in her life had she feared anybody until today. His words were so cold and dark it felt like death.

She went to lock the doors, making sure he was gone. She couldn't even go back to sleep.

***

St. Petersburg, FL

Sama had a beautiful home with three villas that were 24,000 sq. foot spacious with a magnificent sight indoors and outdoors. The soaring, vaulted ceiling was an award-winning look, a spacious covered lanai swimming pool, tropical foliage and a large backyard, seven bedrooms, four bathrooms, upstairs and a private terrace looking out to the backyard oasis. Guards surrounded the home for the Cartel boss. This was one of Sama's homes when he was outside of D.R.

"Boss, she has arrived," one of Sama's security guards said, seeing his boss had been on edge lately.

Julie walked in the living room with a new Birkin bag. "Sama, I was on vacation in Peru. I hope this shit is fucking good. I took my private jet all the way out here." Julie was pissed, slamming her purse on the $50,000 table.

"Julie, we have a big issue. I woke up a sleeping lion," he said, pouring two glasses of red wine.

"Sama, what the hell are you talking about?" Julie looked at him as if he was tripping. She figured he was high on coke.

"Now you with me, I think there are some things I need to tell you," Sama said, taking a gulp of his drink.

"It was too good to be true," she said, knowing he had some bullshit with him. It was just too early for her to peep his game.

"There is a man whose daughter I recently kidnapped when I found out she was the enemy's daughter. The man is a very scary and dangerous man, and we have a long history, but I thought he was dead for years now. Jose Martinez was supposed to kill him, but I hear he is back and this is bad for us both," Sama said.

"Whoa, us? I have nothing to do with this. Why would you kidnap his daughter?" Julie asked.

"I thought he was dead, so I was gonna torture her and kill her, but you are a part of this. He will come for us both, trust me, but that's not all. He is back for something else," Sama said.

"How do you even know all of this shit?"

"He killed a Mexican cartel family in Mexico thinking it was them and he left one person alive to deliver the message to all the big families." Sama was scared to death, looking out his windows.

"Who the fuck is he, Sama?"

"Sombra. Some call him Oscuro."

"That name sounds familiar, but who is he looking for?" Julie tried to think hard about where the name sounded familiar from.

"He's looking for his two sons."

"So?"

"You're not gonna believe this, mami. His sons are Knight and his brother."

Sama saw Julie's face drop to the floor.

Jack Boys vs Dope Boys

***

Hunts Point, Bronx

Knight called an emergency meeting in the factory he owned. Everybody came out alone. Lil K, Behadi, MeMe, and Lit Hound were all there looking at each other. Even Ropes from Atlanta had a seat at the round table, feeling like a boss nigga now. Ropes was in Atlanta, Georgia getting big money since Knight put him on to a bag. He had his city under his wing in a short amount of time.

"We have a few big problems I want to alert everyone on starting with——" Knight paused his speech when he saw a black, handsome older man walk into his factory in a nice black suit. He had good skin and a salt and pepper beard. Everybody pulled out Glocks and aimed it at the man, who was slowly approaching them with his hands up.

"You can lower your weapons."

"Who the fuck are you?" Lil K spoke what was on everybody's mind.

"You two became very handsome young men," the man said, looking back and forth at Knight and Lil K.

"You got two seconds," Knight said, seeing a lot of him in the older gentleman.

"I'm Sombra, your father. I've been here this whole time. Smoke was sent as a double of me to protect my well-being. I will clear that up, but we have a problem. My daughter, y'all sister, was kidnapped from college in Miami and someone has her. I need your help," Sombra said, seeing everyone with a confused look.

To Be Continued
Jack Boys vs Dope Boys 4
Coming Soon

Lock Down Publications and Ca$h Presents assisted
publishing packages.

BASIC PACKAGE $499

Editing

Cover Design

Formatting

UPGRADED PACKAGE $800

Typing

Editing

Cover Design

Formatting

ADVANCE PACKAGE $1,200

Typing

Editing

Cover Design

Formatting

Copyright registration

Proofreading

Upload book to Amazon

LDP SUPREME PACKAGE $1,500

Typing

Editing

Cover Design

Formatting

Copyright registration

Proofreading

Set up Amazon account

Upload book to Amazon

Advertise on LDP Amazon and Facebook page

***Other services available upon request. Additional charges may apply

Lock Down Publications

P.O. Box 944

Stockbridge, GA 30281-9998

Phone # 470 303-9761

Submission Guideline

Submit the first three chapters of your completed manuscript to ldpsubmissions@gmail.com, subject line: Your book's title. The manuscript must be in a .doc file and sent as an attachment. Document should be in Times New Roman, double spaced and in size 12 font. Also, provide your synopsis and full contact information. If sending multiple submissions, they must each be in a separate email.

Have a story but no way to send it electronically? You can still submit to LDP/Ca$h Presents. Send in the first three chapters, written or typed, of your completed manuscript to:

LDP: Submissions Dept
Po Box 944
Stockbridge, Ga 30281

DO NOT send original manuscript. Must be a duplicate.

Provide your synopsis and a cover letter containing your full contact information.

Thanks for considering LDP and Ca$h Presents.

NEW RELEASES

JACK BOYS VS DOPE BOYS 2 by ROMELL TUKES

MURDA WAS THE CASE by ELIJAH R. FREEMAN

KING OF THE TRENCHES 3 by GHOST & TRANAY ADAMS

JACK BOYS VS DOPE BOYS 3 by ROMELL TUKES

Jack Boys vs Dope Boys

STRAIGHT BEAST MODE III

De'Kari

KINGPIN KILLAZ IV

STREET KINGS III

PAID IN BLOOD III

CARTEL KILLAZ IV

DOPE GODS III

Hood Rich

SINS OF A HUSTLA II

ASAD

RICH $AVAGE III

By Martell Troublesome Bolden

YAYO V

Bred In The Game 2

S. Allen

THE STREETS WILL TALK II

By Yolanda Moore

SON OF A DOPE FIEND III

HEAVEN GOT A GHETTO II

SKI MASK MONEY II

By Renta

LOYALTY AIN'T PROMISED III

By Keith Williams

I'M NOTHING WITHOUT HIS LOVE II

SINS OF A THUG II

TO THE THUG I LOVED BEFORE II

IN A HUSTLER I TRUST II

By Monet Dragun

QUIET MONEY IV

EXTENDED CLIP III

Romell Tukes

THUG LIFE IV
By **Trai'Quan**
THE STREETS MADE ME IV
By **Larry D. Wright**
IF YOU CROSS ME ONCE II
ANGEL IV
By **Anthony Fields**
THE STREETS WILL NEVER CLOSE IV
By K'ajji
HARD AND RUTHLESS III
KILLA KOUNTY III
By Khufu
MONEY GAME III
By Smoove Dolla
JACK BOYS VS DOPE BOYS IV
A GANGSTA'S QUR'AN V
COKE GIRLZ II
COKE BOYS II
By Romell Tukes
MURDA WAS THE CASE III
Elijah R. Freeman
THE STREETS NEVER LET GO III
By Robert Baptiste
AN UNFORESEEN LOVE IV
By **Meesha**

MONEY MAFIA II
By **Jibril Williams**
QUEEN OF THE ZOO III
By **Black Migo**

VICIOUS LOYALTY III

By Kingpen

A GANGSTA'S PAIN III

By J-Blunt

CONFESSIONS OF A JACKBOY III

By Nicholas Lock

GRIMEY WAYS III

By Ray Vinci

KING KILLA II

By Vincent "Vitto" Holloway

BETRAYAL OF A THUG II

By Fre$h

THE MURDER QUEENS III

By Michael Gallon

THE BIRTH OF A GANGSTER III

By Delmont Player

TREAL LOVE II

By Le'Monica Jackson

FOR THE LOVE OF BLOOD II

By Jamel Mitchell

RAN OFF ON DA PLUG II

By Paper Boi Rari

HOOD CONSIGLIERE II

By Keese

PRETTY GIRLS DO NASTY THINGS II

By Nicole Goosby

PROTÉGÉ OF A LEGEND II

By Corey Robinson

IT'S JUST ME AND YOU II

By Ah'Million

Romell Tukes

BORN IN THE GRAVE II
By Self Made Tay
FOREVER GANGSTA III
By Adrian Dulan
GORILLAZ IN THE TRENCHES II
By SayNoMore

Available Now

RESTRAINING ORDER **I & II**
By **CA$H & Coffee**
LOVE KNOWS NO BOUNDARIES **I II & III**
By **Coffee**
RAISED AS A GOON I, II, III & IV
BRED BY THE SLUMS I, II, III
BLAST FOR ME I & II
ROTTEN TO THE CORE I II III
A BRONX TALE I, II, III
DUFFLE BAG CARTEL I II III IV V VI
HEARTLESS GOON I II III IV V
A SAVAGE DOPEBOY I II
DRUG LORDS I II III
CUTTHROAT MAFIA I II
KING OF THE TRENCHES

Jack Boys vs Dope Boys

By **Ghost**
LAY IT DOWN **I & II**
LAST OF A DYING BREED I II
BLOOD STAINS OF A SHOTTA I & II III
By **Jamaica**
LOYAL TO THE GAME I II III
LIFE OF SIN I, II III
By **TJ & Jelissa**
BLOODY COMMAS I & II
SKI MASK CARTEL I II & III
KING OF NEW YORK I II,III IV V
RISE TO POWER I II III
COKE KINGS I II III IV V
BORN HEARTLESS I II III IV
KING OF THE TRAP I II
By **T.J. Edwards**
IF LOVING HIM IS WRONG...I & II
LOVE ME EVEN WHEN IT HURTS I II III
By **Jelissa**
WHEN THE STREETS CLAP BACK I & II III
THE HEART OF A SAVAGE I II III IV
MONEY MAFIA
LOYAL TO THE SOIL I II III
By **Jibril Williams**
A DISTINGUISHED THUG STOLE MY HEART I II & III
LOVE SHOULDN'T HURT I II III IV
RENEGADE BOYS I II III IV
PAID IN KARMA I II III
SAVAGE STORMS I II III
AN UNFORESEEN LOVE I II III

Romell Tukes

By **Meesha**

A GANGSTER'S CODE I &, II III

A GANGSTER'S SYN I II III

THE SAVAGE LIFE I II III

CHAINED TO THE STREETS I II III

BLOOD ON THE MONEY I II III

A GANGSTA'S PAIN I II

By J-Blunt

PUSH IT TO THE LIMIT

By **Bre' Hayes**

BLOOD OF A BOSS **I, II, III, IV, V**

SHADOWS OF THE GAME

TRAP BASTARD

By **Askari**

THE STREETS BLEED MURDER **I, II & III**

THE HEART OF A GANGSTA I II& III

By **Jerry Jackson**

CUM FOR ME I II III IV V VI VII VIII

An **LDP Erotica Collaboration**

BRIDE OF A HUSTLA **I II & II**

THE FETTI GIRLS **I, II& III**

CORRUPTED BY A GANGSTA I, II III, IV

BLINDED BY HIS LOVE

THE PRICE YOU PAY FOR LOVE I, II ,III

DOPE GIRL MAGIC I II III

By **Destiny Skai**

WHEN A GOOD GIRL GOES BAD

By **Adrienne**

THE COST OF LOYALTY I II III

By Kweli

Jack Boys vs Dope Boys

A GANGSTER'S REVENGE **I II III & IV**

THE BOSS MAN'S DAUGHTERS I II III IV V

A SAVAGE LOVE **I & II**

BAE BELONGS TO ME I II

A HUSTLER'S DECEIT I, II, III

WHAT BAD BITCHES DO I, II, III

SOUL OF A MONSTER I II III

KILL ZONE

A DOPE BOY'S QUEEN I II III

TIL DEATH

By **Aryanna**

A KINGPIN'S AMBITON

A KINGPIN'S AMBITION **II**

I MURDER FOR THE DOUGH

By **Ambitious**

TRUE SAVAGE I II III IV V VI VII

DOPE BOY MAGIC I, II, III

MIDNIGHT CARTEL I II III

CITY OF KINGZ I II

NIGHTMARE ON SILENT AVE

THE PLUG OF LIL MEXICO II

CLASSIC CITY

By **Chris Green**

A DOPEBOY'S PRAYER

By **Eddie "Wolf" Lee**

THE KING CARTEL **I, II & III**

By **Frank Gresham**

THESE NIGGAS AIN'T LOYAL **I, II & III**

By **Nikki Tee**

GANGSTA SHYT **I II &III**

By **CATO**

THE ULTIMATE BETRAYAL

By **Phoenix**

BOSS'N UP **I , II & III**

By **Royal Nicole**

I LOVE YOU TO DEATH

By **Destiny J**

I RIDE FOR MY HITTA

I STILL RIDE FOR MY HITTA

By **Misty Holt**

LOVE & CHASIN' PAPER

By **Qay Crockett**

TO DIE IN VAIN

SINS OF A HUSTLA

By **ASAD**

BROOKLYN HUSTLAZ

By **Boogsy Morina**

BROOKLYN ON LOCK I & II

By **Sonovia**

GANGSTA CITY

By **Teddy Duke**

A DRUG KING AND HIS DIAMOND I & II III

A DOPEMAN'S RICHES

HER MAN, MINE'S TOO I, II

CASH MONEY HO'S

THE WIFEY I USED TO BE I II

PRETTY GIRLS DO NASTY THINGS

By Nicole Goosby

TRAPHOUSE KING **I II & III**

KINGPIN KILLAZ I II III

Jack Boys vs Dope Boys

STREET KINGS I II

PAID IN BLOOD **I II**

CARTEL KILLAZ I II III

DOPE GODS I II

By **Hood Rich**

LIPSTICK KILLAH **I, II, III**

CRIME OF PASSION I II & III

FRIEND OR FOE I II III

By **Mimi**

STEADY MOBBN' **I, II, III**

THE STREETS STAINED MY SOUL I II III

By **Marcellus Allen**

WHO SHOT YA **I, II, III**

SON OF A DOPE FIEND I II

HEAVEN GOT A GHETTO

SKI MASK MONEY

Renta

GORILLAZ IN THE BAY **I II III IV**

TEARS OF A GANGSTA I II

3X KRAZY I II

STRAIGHT BEAST MODE I II

DE'KARI

TRIGGADALE I II III

MURDAROBER WAS THE CASE I II

Elijah R. Freeman

GOD BLESS THE TRAPPERS I, II, III

THESE SCANDALOUS STREETS I, II, III

FEAR MY GANGSTA I, II, III IV, V

THESE STREETS DON'T LOVE NOBODY I, II

BURY ME A G I, II, III, IV, V

Jack Boys vs Dope Boys

GLOCKS ON SATIN SHEETS I II
By Adrian Dulan
TOE TAGZ I II III IV
LEVELS TO THIS SHYT I II
IT'S JUST ME AND YOU
By Ah'Million
KINGPIN DREAMS I II III
RAN OFF ON DA PLUG
By Paper Boi Rari
CONFESSIONS OF A GANGSTA I II III IV
CONFESSIONS OF A JACKBOY I II
By Nicholas Lock
I'M NOTHING WITHOUT HIS LOVE
SINS OF A THUG
TO THE THUG I LOVED BEFORE
A GANGSTA SAVED XMAS
IN A HUSTLER I TRUST
By Monet Dragun
CAUGHT UP IN THE LIFE I II III
THE STREETS NEVER LET GO I II
By Robert Baptiste
NEW TO THE GAME I II III
MONEY, MURDER & MEMORIES I II III
By **Malik D. Rice**
LIFE OF A SAVAGE I II III
A GANGSTA'S QUR'AN I II III IV
MURDA SEASON I II III
GANGLAND CARTEL I II III
CHI'RAQ GANGSTAS I II III
KILLERS ON ELM STREET I II III

255

JACK BOYZ N DA BRONX I II III

A DOPEBOY'S DREAM I II III

JACK BOYS VS DOPE BOYS I II III

COKE GIRLZ

COKE BOYS

By Romell Tukes

LOYALTY AIN'T PROMISED I II

By Keith Williams

QUIET MONEY I II III

THUG LIFE I II III

EXTENDED CLIP I II

A GANGSTA'S PARADISE

By **Trai'Quan**

THE STREETS MADE ME I II III

By **Larry D. Wright**

THE ULTIMATE SACRIFICE I, II, III, IV, V, VI

KHADIFI

IF YOU CROSS ME ONCE

ANGEL I II III

IN THE BLINK OF AN EYE

By **Anthony Fields**

THE LIFE OF A HOOD STAR

By Ca$h & Rashia Wilson

THE STREETS WILL NEVER CLOSE I II III

By K'ajji

CREAM I II III

THE STREETS WILL TALK

By Yolanda Moore

NIGHTMARES OF A HUSTLA I II III

By King Dream

Jack Boys vs Dope Boys

CONCRETE KILLA I II III

VICIOUS LOYALTY I II

By Kingpen

HARD AND RUTHLESS I II

MOB TOWN 251

THE BILLIONAIRE BENTLEYS I II III

By Von Diesel

GHOST MOB

Stilloan Robinson

MOB TIES I II III IV V VI

SOUL OF A HUSTLER, HEART OF A KILLER

GORILLAZ IN THE TRENCHES

By SayNoMore

BODYMORE MURDERLAND I II III

THE BIRTH OF A GANGSTER I II

By Delmont Player

FOR THE LOVE OF A BOSS

By C. D. Blue

MOBBED UP I II III IV

THE BRICK MAN I II III IV

THE COCAINE PRINCESS I II III IV V

By King Rio

KILLA KOUNTY I II III

By Khufu

MONEY GAME I II

By Smoove Dolla

A GANGSTA'S KARMA I II

By FLAME

KING OF THE TRENCHES I II III

by **GHOST & TRANAY ADAMS**

QUEEN OF THE ZOO I II
By **Black Migo**
GRIMEY WAYS I II
By **Ray Vinci**
XMAS WITH AN ATL SHOOTER
By **Ca$h & Destiny Skai**
KING KILLA
By **Vincent "Vitto" Holloway**
BETRAYAL OF A THUG
By **Fre$h**
THE MURDER QUEENS I II
By **Michael Gallon**
TREAL LOVE
By **Le'Monica Jackson**
FOR THE LOVE OF BLOOD
By **Jamel Mitchell**
HOOD CONSIGLIERE
By **Keese**
PROTÉGÉ OF A LEGEND
By **Corey Robinson**
BORN IN THE GRAVE
By **Self Made Tay**
MOAN IN MY MOUTH
By **XTASY**

Jack Boys vs Dope Boys

<u>BOOKS BY LDP'S CEO, CA$H</u>

TRUST IN NO MAN

TRUST IN NO MAN 2

TRUST IN NO MAN 3

BONDED BY BLOOD

SHORTY GOT A THUG

THUGS CRY

THUGS CRY 2

THUGS CRY 3

TRUST NO BITCH

TRUST NO BITCH 2

TRUST NO BITCH 3

TIL MY CASKET DROPS

RESTRAINING ORDER

RESTRAINING ORDER 2

IN LOVE WITH A CONVICT

LIFE OF A HOOD STAR

XMAS WITH AN ATL SHOOTER

Romell Tukes